FLY ALREADY

FLY ALREADY

ETGAR KERET

TRANSLATED BY

Sondra Silverston

Nathan Englander

Jessica Cohen

Miriam Shlesinger

Yardenne Greenspan

RIVERHEAD BOOKS · NEW YORK · 2019

RIVERHEAD BOOKS
An imprint of Penguin Random House LLC
penguinrandomhouse.com

Originally published, in Hebrew and in somewhat different form,
as *A Glitch at the Edge of the Galaxy*, by Kinneret Zmora-Bitan Dvir, 2018
First American edition published by Riverhead Books, 2019
Published by arrangement with the author and
the Institute for the Translation of Hebrew Literature

The following stories were previously published in English: "Fly Already,"
"One Gram Short," and "To the Moon and Back" in *The New Yorker*; "Todd" on Electric
Literature; "Tabula Rasa" (as "A: Only Through Death Will You Learn Your True Identity") on
Wired; "Car Concentrate" in *Granta*; "At Night," "GooDeed," and "Crumb Cake" in *McSweeney's*;
"Windows" in *Playboy*; "Dad with Mashed Potatoes" in *Zoetrope: All-Story*; "Arctic Lizard" on
BuzzFeed; "Ladder" in *Tin House*; "Allergies" in *Tel Aviv Noir*, edited by Etgar Keret and Assaf
Gavron (Akashic Books); and "Chips" on Nerve. "Evolution of a Breakup" was read on the internet
version of an episode of *This American Life* on National Public Radio. "Yad Vashem"
is published in English for the first time in this volume.

All stories in this volume were translated by Sondra Silverston, except for "One Gram Short,"
"Car Concentrate," translated by Nathan Englander; "Arctic Lizard," "Pineapple Crush,"
"Evolution of a Breakup," translated by Jessica Cohen; "Yad Vashem," translated by
Miriam Shlesinger; "Allergies," translated by Yardenne Greenspan.

Library of Congress Cataloging-in-Publication Data

Names: Keret, Etgar, 1967– author. | Silverston, Sondra, translator. |
Englander, Nathan, translator. | Cohen, Jessica, translator. |
Shlesinger, Miriam, 1947– translator. | Greenspan, Yardenne, translator.
Title: Fly already / Etgar Keret; translated by Sondra Silverston,
Nathan Englander, Jessica Cohen, Miriam Shlesinger, Yardenne Greenspan.
Description: New York: Riverhead Books, 2019
Identifiers: LCCN 2018040497 (print) | LCCN 2018042215 (ebook) |
ISBN 9780698166110 (ebook) | ISBN 9781594633270 (hardcover)
Classification: LCC PJ5054.K375 (ebook) | LCC PJ5054.K375 A2 2019 (print) |
DDC 892.43/6—dc23
LC record available at https://lccn.loc.gov/2018040497

BOOK DESIGN BY LUCIA BERNARD

Printed in Canada
1   3   5   7   9   10   8   6   4   2

For Eli and Guy

CONTENTS

FLY ALREADY

FLY ALREADY

———•————•———

P.T. sees him first. We're on our way to the park to play ball when he suddenly says, "Daddy, look!" His head is tilted back and he's squinting hard to see something far above me, and before I can even begin to imagine an alien spaceship or a piano about to fall on our heads, my gut tells me that something really bad is happening here. But when I turn to see what P.T. is looking at, all I notice is an ugly, four-story building covered in plaster and air conditioners, as if it has some kind of skin disease. The sun is sitting directly on it, slightly blinding me, and as I'm trying to get a better angle, I hear P.T. say, "He wants to fly." Now I can see a guy in a white button-down shirt standing on the roof railing looking straight at me, and behind me, P.T. whispers, "Is he a superhero?" But instead of answering him, I shout at the guy, "Don't do it!"

The guy stares at me and doesn't answer. I shout at him again, "Don't do it, please! Whatever brought you up there must seem like something you'll never get over, but believe me, you will. If you jump now, you'll leave this world with that dead-end feeling. That'll be your last memory of life. Not family, not love—only defeat. But if you stay, I swear to you by everything I hold dear that your pain will start to fade, and in a few years, the only thing left will be a weird story you tell people over a beer. A story about how you once wanted to jump off a roof and some guy standing below shouted at you . . ."

"What?" the guy on the roof yells back at me, pointing at his ear. He probably can't hear me because of the noise coming from the road. Or maybe it isn't the noise, because I heard his "What?" perfectly well. Maybe he's just hard of hearing. P.T., who's hugging my thighs without being able to encircle them completely, as if I were some kind of giant baobab tree, yells at the guy, "Do you have superpowers?" but the guy points at his ear again as if to say he can't hear, and shouts, "I'm sick of it! Enough! How much can I take?" P.T. shouts back at him, as if they were having the most ordinary conversation in the world, "Come on, fly already!" And I'm starting to feel that stress, the stress that comes with knowing that it's all on you.

I have it a lot at work. With the family too, but not as much. Like what happened on the way to Lake Kinneret, when I tried to brake and the tires locked. The car started to skid along the road and I said to myself, "Either you fix this or it's all over." That time, driving to the Dead Sea, I didn't fix it, and Liat, the only one not buckled in, died, and I was left alone with the kids.

P.T. was two and barely knew how to speak, but Amit never stopped asking me, "When is Mommy coming back? When is Mommy coming back?" and I'm talking about *after* the funeral. He was eight then, an age when you're supposed to understand what it means when someone dies, but he kept asking. And even without the constant, annoying questions, I knew that everything was my fault and wanted to end it all. Just like the guy on the roof. But here I am today, walking without crutches, living with 3Imona, a good dad. I want to tell the guy on the roof all about it, I want to tell him that I know exactly how he feels right now, and that if he doesn't flatten himself like a pizza on the sidewalk, it'll pass. I know what I'm talking about, because no one on this blue planet was as miserable as I was. He just has to get down from there and give himself a week. A month. Even a year, if necessary.

But how can you say all that to a guy who's half deaf? Meanwhile, P.T. pulls my hand and says, "He's not going to fly today anyway, Daddy, let's go to the park before it gets dark." But I stay where I am and shout as loudly as I can, "People die like flies all the time, even without killing themselves. Don't do it! Please don't do it!" The guy on the roof nods—it looks like this time, he heard something—and shouts back at me, "How did you know? How did you know she died?" Someone always dies, I want to yell back at him. Always. If not her, then someone else. But that won't get him down from there, so instead I shout, "There's a kid here," and point at P.T., "he doesn't need to see this." Then P.T. yells, "Yes I do! Yes I do! Come on and fly already, before it gets dark!" It's December, and it really does get dark early.

If he jumps, that'll be on my conscience, too. Irena the psychologist at the clinic will give me that "After you I'm going home" look of hers and say, "You're not responsible for everyone. You have to get that into your head." And I'll nod, because I know that the session ends in two minutes and she has to pick up her daughter from day care, but it won't change anything because I'll have to carry that half-deaf guy on my back, along with Liat and Amit's glass eye. I have to save him. "Wait there for me!" I scream as loudly as I can. "I'm coming up to talk to you!"

"I can't go on without her. I can't!" he shouts. "Wait a minute," I yell, and say to P.T., "Come on, sweetie, let's go up to the roof." P.T. gives an adorable shake of his head, the way he always does right before he sticks the knife in, and says, "If he flies, we can see better from here."

"He won't fly," I say, "not today. Let's go up there just for a minute. Daddy has to tell the man something." But P.T. persists. "So yell from here." His arm slips out of my grasp and he throws himself down on the ground, the way he likes to do to Simona and me at the mall. "Let's race to the roof," I say. "If we get there without stopping, P.T. and Daddy get ice cream as a prize."

"Ice cream now," P.T. wails, rolling around on the sidewalk, "ice cream now!" I have no time for this crap. I pick him up. He squirms and screams, but I ignore it and start running toward the building.

"What happened to the kid?" I hear the guy shout from the roof. I don't answer, and race into the building. Maybe his curiosity will stop him for now. Maybe it'll keep him from jumping long enough for me to get up to the roof.

The kid is heavy. It's hard to climb all those stairs when you're holding a five-and-a-half-year-old kid in your arms, especially one who doesn't want to go up the stairs. By the third floor, I'm completely out of breath. A fat redhead who must have heard P.T.'s screams opens her door a crack and asks who I'm looking for, but I ignore her and keep climbing. Even if I want to say something to her, I don't have enough air in my lungs.

"No one lives upstairs," she shouts after me, "it's just the roof." When she says "roof," her shrill voice breaks and P.T. yells back at her in a tear-filled voice, "Ice cream now! Now!" I don't have a free hand to push open the door that should lead outside—my arms are full of P.T., who doesn't stop flailing—so I kick it as hard as I can. The roof is empty. The guy who was on the railing a minute ago isn't there anymore. He didn't wait for us. Didn't wait to find out why the kid was screaming.

"He flew," P.T. sobs, "he flew and because of you we didn't see anything!" I start walking toward the railing. Maybe he changed his mind and went back into the building, I try to tell myself. But I don't believe it. I know he's down there, his body sprawled on the sidewalk at an unnatural angle. I know it, and I have a kid in my arms who absolutely should not see that because it'll traumatize him for the rest of his life, and he's already been through enough. But my legs take me to the edge of the roof. It's like scratching a wound, like ordering another shot of Chivas when you know you've already had too much to drink, like driving a car when you know you're tired, so tired.

Now that we're right at the railing, we start to feel the height. P.T. stops crying and I can hear both of us panting and the ambulance siren in the distance. It seems to be asking me, "Why? Why do you need to see it? You think it'll change anything? Make anyone feel better?" Suddenly, the redhead's shrill voice commands me from behind, "Put him down!" I turn around, not really understanding what she wants. "Put me down," P.T. shouts, too. It always gets him going when a stranger butts in.

"He's just a kid," the redhead keeps saying, but her voice is suddenly cracked and soft. She's on the verge of tears. The sound of the siren is getting closer and the redhead starts walking toward me. "I know you're suffering," she says, "I know that everything is so hard. I know, believe me." There's so much pain in her voice that even P.T. stops flailing and stares at her, mesmerized. "Look at me," she whispers, "fat, alone. I had a child once, too. You know what it is to lose a child? Do you have any idea of what you're about to do?" Still in my arms, P.T. hugs me tight. "Look at what a sweet child he is," she says, already close to us, her thick hand stroking P.T.'s hair.

"There was a man here," P.T. says, fixing his huge green eyes, Liat's eyes, on her. "There was a man here, but now he flew away. And because of Daddy, we didn't see him." The siren stops right under us and I take another step toward the railing, but the redhead's sweaty hand grabs mine—"Don't do it," she says, "please, don't do it."

P.T. has a scoop of vanilla in a plastic cup. I order pistachio and chocolate chip in a cone. The redhead asks for a chocolate milk shake. All the tables in the ice cream parlor are filthy, so I clean one for us. P.T. insists on tasting the milkshake and she lets him. She's called Liat, too. It's a common name. She doesn't know about our Liat, about the accident; she doesn't know anything about us. And I don't know anything about her. Except that she lost her kid. When we left the building, they were putting the guy's body into the ambulance. Luckily, it was covered with a white sheet. One less image of a corpse in my mind. The ice cream is too sweet for me, but P.T. and the redhead look happy. With his cone in one hand, he reaches out for her milkshake with the other. I don't know why he always does that; after all, he's still eating his ice cream, why does he need more? I open my mouth to say something to him, but the redhead signals that it's okay and gives him her almost empty cup. Her son's dead, my wife's dead, the guy on the roof is dead. "He's so cute," she whispers as P.T. strains to suck up the last drop of milkshake in the paper cup. He really is cute.

ONE GRAM SHORT

There's an adorable waitress at the coffee shop next to my house. Benny, who works in the kitchen, told me that she doesn't have a boyfriend, that her name is Shikma, and that she is a fan of recreational drugs. Before she started working there, I'd never been in the place—not even once. But now you can find me perched at a table every morning. Drinking espresso. Talking to her a little. About things I read in the paper, about the other people sitting in the shop, about cookies. Sometimes, I even manage to make her laugh. And when she laughs, it does me good. I've already almost invited her to a movie a bunch of times. But a movie is just too in-your-face. A movie is one step before dinner in a restaurant or asking her to fly off for a weekend in Sinai. A movie isn't something you can interpret in a number of ways. It's just like saying, "I want you." And if she isn't interested and says no, the whole thing ends in unpleasantness. Because of that, I thought asking her to smoke a joint would be better. At most she'll say, "I don't smoke," and I'll make some joke about stoners, and, like it's nothing, order another short espresso and move on.

Because of that, I call Avri. Avri is maybe the only one from my high school class who was a super-heavy smoker. It's been more than two years since the last time we spoke. I run through small talk in my head as I dial, hunting for something I can talk to him about before I ask about the weed. But just as I'm asking him how he's doing, Avri immediately says, "Dry. They closed the Lebanese border on us because of the trouble in Syria, and the one with Egypt because of all that al-Qaeda shit. There's nothing to smoke, my brother. I'm climbing the walls." I ask him what else is going on, and he answers me, even though we both know I'm not interested. He tells me his girlfriend is pregnant, and that they both want the kid, and that his girlfriend's mother is a widow and not only is pressuring them to get married but wants a religious ceremony—because that's what his girlfriend's father would have wanted if he were still alive. I mean, go try and stand up to an argument like that! What can you do? Dig up the father with a backhoe and ask him? And all this time that Avri's talking, I'm trying to get him to relax, telling him it's no big deal. Because for me, it really isn't so terrible whether Avri gets married in front of a rabbi or not. Even if he decides he's going to leave the country for good or have a sex change, I'm going to take it in stride. But of all things, it's that bud for Shikma that's important to me. So I throw this out there: "Dude, someone somewhere has some product, right?

It's not for the high, it's for a girl. Someone special I want to impress." "Dry," Avri says again. "I swear to you, I've even started smoking Spice like some kind of junkie." "I can't bring her that synthetic shit," I tell him. "It won't look good." "I know," he mumbles from the other end of the line, "I know, but right now, weed—there just isn't any."

Two days later, Avri calls me in the morning and tells me that maybe he has something, but it's complicated. I tell him I'm ready to pay for the expensive stuff. This is a onetime thing for me, special, and I hardly need a gram. "I didn't say 'expensive,'" he says, annoyed, "I said 'complicated.' Meet me in forty minutes at 46 Carlebach Street and I'll explain."

"Complicated" is not what I need right now. And from what I remember back in high school, Avri's "complicateds" are complicated indeed. All in all, I'm just after a single bud, even just one joint, to smoke with a pretty girl who laughs at my jokes. I don't have the headspace right now for a meeting with hardened criminals or whoever it is that lives over on Carlebach. Avri's tone on the telephone is enough to stress me out, and also he said "complicated" twice. When I get to the address, he's already waiting. And he's still got the helmet from his scooter sitting on his head. "This guy," he says to me, panting on the stairs, "the one we're headed up to now, he's a lawyer. My friend cleans his house every week, but not for money—she does it for medical marijuana. He's got a bad cancer of the something—I'm not sure which part—and he's got a prescription for forty grams a month but can barely smoke it. I asked her to ask him if he maybe wants to lighten his load a little, and he said he'd discuss it but insisted that two people come, I don't know why. So I picked up the phone and called you." "Avri," I say to him, "I asked for a bud, I don't want to go to some drug deal with a lawyer you've never met before in your life." "It's not a deal," Avri says to me, "it's just a person who requested that two of us stop by his apartment to talk. If he says something to us that doesn't sit right, we say good-bye immediately and cut loose. In any case, there won't be a deal today. I don't have a shekel on me. At most, we'll know we've got things rolling."

I still don't feel good about it. Not because I think it'll be dangerous. But because I'm afraid it'll be unpleasant. I just can't handle unpleasant. To sit with unfamiliar people in unfamiliar houses, with that kind of heavy atmosphere looming. It does me bad. "*Nu,*" Avri says, "just go up, and after two minutes make like you got a text and have to run. Don't leave me hanging. He asked that two people show up. So walk into the house with me so I don't come off like an idiot, and one minute after that, just split." It still won't sit right, but when Avri puts it that way, it's hard for me to say no without coming off like a dick.

The lawyer's last name is Corman, or at the least that's what's written on the door. And the guy's actually all right. He offers us Cokes and puts a lemon wedge in each glass with some ice, like we're in the lobby of a hotel. And his apartment's all right, too: bright, and it even smells good. "Look," he says, "I've got to be in court in an hour. A civil suit over a hit-

and-run involving a ten-year-old girl. The driver barely did a year in jail, and now I'm representing the parents, who are suing him for two million. He's an Arab, the one that hit her, but from a rich family." "Wow," Avri says, as if he has any idea what this Corman is actually talking about, "but we're here about a completely different matter. We're Tina's friends. The subject we came to discuss is weed." "It's the same subject," Corman says, impatient. "If you give me a chance to finish, you'll understand. In this case, the family of the driver is going to come out in numbers to show their support. On the side of the dead girl, outside of her parents, not another soul is going to show. And the parents are just going to sit there silently with their heads bowed, not saying a word." Avri nods and goes quiet. He still doesn't understand but doesn't want to aggravate Corman. "I want you and your friend here to come to court, acting like you're related to the victim, and make a ruckus. Make some noise. Scream at the defendant, call him a murderer. Maybe cry, curse a bit, but nothing racist, just, 'You piece of shit' and things of that nature. In short, they should feel your presence. They need to understand that there are people in this city who feel he's getting off cheap. It may sound stupid to you, but things like that affect judges deeply. It shakes them up a little, shakes the mothballs from those old, dry laws, rubs the judges up against the real world." "About the weed?" Avri tries. "I'm getting to that just now," Corman cuts him off. "Give me that half hour in court and I'll give each of you ten grams. If you scream loud enough, maybe even fifteen. What do you say?" "I just need a gram," I tell him. "How about you sell it to me, and we call it a day? After that, you and Avri . . ." "Sell?" Corman laughs. "For money? What am I, a dealer? I may give a baggie to a friend here and there as a little present." "So give *me* a present," I beg. "It's a fucking gram!" "But what did I just say a second ago?" Corman smiles an unpleasant smile. "I'll give. First, just prove to me that you're really a friend."

If it wasn't Avri, I'd never agree, but he keeps telling me that this is our chance and that it's not like we were doing something dangerous or breaking the law. Smoking dope is against the law, but screaming at someone who ran over a little girl—that's not only legal, it's downright normative. "Who knows," he says, "if there are cameras there, they might even see us on the nightly news." "But what's the deal with pretending like we're family?" I keep saying. "I mean, the girl's parents will know we're not related." "He didn't tell us to say we're related," Avri says, in defense of Corman. "He just said that we should scream. If anyone asks, we can always tell them that we read it in the paper and we're just citizens who are truly engaged."

We're having this conversation in the courthouse lobby, even though it's sunny outside. Inside it's dark and smells like some mix of sewage and mildew. And even though Avri and I keep on arguing, it's long been clear to both of us that I'm already in. If I weren't, I wouldn't have come here with him on the back of the scooter. "Don't worry," he says to me, "I'll scream for us both. You don't have to do anything, just act like you're a friend that's trying hard to calm me down. Just so they feel that you're with me." The reason Avri tells me that I don't have to scream is because half the driver's family is already there, staring us down in the lobby. The driver himself is chubby and looks really young, and he talks to every new person who arrives, kissing them all, like it's a wedding. At the plaintiff's table, next to Corman and another young lawyer with a beard, sit the parents of the girl. They don't look like they're at a wedding. They look wiped out. The mother is maybe fifty or older but small, like a tiny bird. She has short gray hair and looks completely neurotic. The father sits there with his eyes closed. Every once in a while he opens them, and after a second closes them again.

The proceedings begin, and it looks like we've come at the end of some complicated process, and everything sounds kind of technical and fragmented. They just keep murmuring the numbers of different sections and articles. I try to picture Shikma and me sitting here in court, after our daughter has been run over. We're destroyed, but we're supporting each other, and then she whispers in my ear, "I want that fucking murderer to pay." It's not fun to imagine, so I stop and instead start to imagine the two of us in my apartment, smoking something and watching some National Geographic documentary about animals, with the TV on mute. Somehow we suddenly start making out, and when she clings to me with a kiss, I feel her chest crushed up against mine . . . "Hyena!" Avri jumps up in the gallery and starts yelling. "What are you smiling at? You killed a little girl. Standing there in your polo shirt like you're on a cruise—they should let you rot behind bars."

Some of the relatives from the driver's family start coming in our direction, and I stand up and act like I'm trying to calm Avri down. Actually, I'm trying to calm Avri down. The judge bangs his gavel and calls on Avri to come to order. He says that if Avri doesn't stop screaming, the court officers will toss him out by force, which at the moment sounds like a far more pleasant option than interacting with the driver's entire family, a few of whom are now standing an inch from my face and cursing, and shoving Avri.

"Terrorist!" Avri shrieks. "You deserve the death penalty." I've got no idea why he says that. But one guy, with a huge mustache, slaps him. I try to separate them, to get between him and Avri, and catch a head butt to the face. The court officers drag Avri out. On the way, he gets in one last "You killed a little girl. You plucked a flower. If only they'd murder your daughter, too." By the time he says that, I'm already on the floor, on all fours. Blood runs from my nose or from my forehead, I'm not exactly sure where it's dripping from. Right when Avri is delivering the bit about the driver's daughter being killed as well, someone lands a real good, solid kick to my ribs.

As soon as we get back to Corman's house, he opens the freezer and gives me a bag of frozen peas and tells me to press hard. Avri doesn't say a thing to him or to me, just asks where the weed is. "Why did you say terrorist?" Corman asks. "I told you specifically not to mention that he's an Arab." "'Terrorist' is not anti-Arab," Avri says, defensive. "It's like 'murderer.' The settlers also have terrorists." Corman doesn't say anything to him, he just goes into the bathroom and comes out with two little plastic bags. He hands me one and throws the other to Avri, who nearly fumbles the catch. "There's twenty in each one," Corman says to me as he opens the front door. "You can take the peas with you."

The next morning at the café, Shikma asks what happened to my face. I tell her it was an accident. I went to visit a married friend and slipped on his kid's toy on the living room floor. "And I was already thinking that you got beat up over a girl," Shikma says, laughing, and brings me my espresso. "That also happens sometimes." I try to smile back. "Hang around with me long enough and you'll see me get beat up over girls and over friends and defending kittens. But it'll always be me getting beat up, never doing the beating." "You're just like my brother," Shikma says, and continues to laugh. "The kind of guy who breaks up the fight and ends up getting hit." I can feel the plastic bag with the twenty grams rustling in my coat pocket. But instead of paying attention to it, I ask her if she's had a chance to see that new movie about the astronaut whose satellite blows up, leaving her stranded in outer space with George Clooney. She says no and asks me what that has to do with what we're talking about. "Nothing," I confess, "but it sounds pretty awesome. It's three-D, with the glasses and everything. Do you maybe want to go see it with me?"

There's a moment of silence, and I know that after it passes, the yes or the no will come. In that moment, the image pops back into my head. Shikma crying. The two of us in court, holding hands. I try to change channels, to switch to the other image, the two of us, together, kissing on my torn living room couch. Try, and fail. That picture, I just can't shake it.

THE NEXT-TO-LAST TIME
I WAS SHOT OUT OF A CANNON

The next-to-last time I was shot out of a cannon was when Odelia left with the kid. I was working as a cage cleaner for the Romanian Circus, which was in town. I finished the lions' cages in half an hour, and also the bears' cages, but the elephants' cages were really a killer. My back hurt and the whole world smelled of shit. My life was ruined and the smell of shit fit perfectly. I needed a break, so I grabbed myself a corner outside the cage and rolled a cigarette. I didn't even wash my hands before doing it.

After a couple of drags, I heard a small, fake cough behind me. It was the circus manager. His name was Roman, and he had won the circus in a card game. The old Romanian who originally owned the circus was holding three queens, but Roman had four of a kind. He told me the story the day he hired me. "Who needs luck," he said with a wink, "when you know how to cheat." I was sure Roman would make a scene because I was taking a break in the middle of work, but he didn't even look angry. "Tell me," he said, "you want to make an easy thousand?" I nodded, and he went on, "I just saw Ishtevan, our human cannonball, in his caravan. He's completely smashed. I couldn't wake him up and his show's supposed to start in fifteen minutes . . ." Roman's open hand drew the route of a cannonball in the air, ending with his squat fingers banging against my forehead, "I give you a thousand in cash if you take his place."

"I've never been shot out of a cannon," I said and took another drag of my cigarette. "Sure you have," Roman said, "when your ex left you, when your son told you he hates you, when your fat cat ran away. Listen, to be a human cannonball, you don't need to be flexible or fast or strong, just lonely and miserable as hell."

"I'm not lonely," I protested. "Really?" Roman laughed. "So tell me—never mind sex, when was the last time someone even smiled at you?"

Before the show, they dressed me in silver overalls. I asked an old clown with a giant red nose if I didn't need some instruction before they shot me. "The important thing," he mumbled, "is to relax your body. Or contract it, one or the other. I don't remember exactly. And you have to make sure the cannon is pointed straight ahead so it doesn't miss the target."

"And that's it?" I asked. Even in the silver overalls, I still stank of elephant shit. The circus manager came over and slapped me on the back. "Remember," he said, "after they shoot you at the target, you get straight back to the stage, smile, and bow. And if, God forbid, something hurts or even if you break something, you have to keep it in, you have to hide it so the audience doesn't see."

The people in the audience looked really happy. They cheered for the clowns that pushed me into the mouth of the cannon, and a second before the fuse was lit, the fat clown with the flower that sprayed water asked me, "You're sure you want to do this? It's the last chance to change your mind." I nodded, and he said, "You know that Ishtevan, the last human cannon-ball, is in the hospital now with ten broken ribs?"

"He isn't," I said, "he's just a little drunk. He's sleeping in his caravan now."

"Whatever you say," the fat clown sighed, and struck the match.

Looking back, I have to admit that the angle of the cannon was too sharp. Instead of hitting the target, I flew upward, made a hole in the top of the tent, and continued flying to the sky, way up high. I flew over the abandoned drive-in theater where Odelia and I once used to go to see movies. I flew over the playground where a few dog owners walked around with rustling plastic bags. Little Max was there too, playing ball, and when I flew over him, he looked up, smiled, and waved hello. On Yarkon Street, behind the place where the American em-bassy keeps its dumpsters, I saw Tiger, my fat cat, trying to catch a pigeon. A few seconds later, when I landed in the water, the handful of people on the beach stood up and applauded for me, and when I came out of the water, a tall girl with a nose ring handed me her towel and smiled.

When I came back to the circus, my clothes were still wet and everything was dark. The tent was empty, and in the middle of it, near the cannon I was shot out of, Roman was counting the day's take. "You missed the target," he grumbled, "and you didn't come back to bow like we agreed. I'm deducting four hundred for that." He handed me a few wrinkled bills, and when he saw I wasn't taking them, he gave me a tough east European look and said, "If I were you, I'd take it."

"Forget the money, Roman," I said, and walked over to the mouth of the cannon, "Do a friend a favor and shoot me out again."

TODD

——•—————————•——

My friend Todd wants me to write him a story that will help him get girls into bed.

"You've already written stories that make girls cry," he says. "And ones that make them laugh. So now write one that'll make them jump into bed with me."

I try to explain to him that it doesn't work that way. True, there are some girls who cry when they read my stories, and there are some guys who—

"Forget guys," Todd interrupts. "Guys don't do it for me. I'm telling you this up front, so you won't write a story that'll get anyone who reads it into my bed, just girls. I'm telling you this to avoid unpleasantness."

So I explain to him again, in my patient tone, that it doesn't work that way. A story isn't a magic spell or hypnotherapy; a story is just a way to share with other people something you feel, something intimate, sometimes even embarrassing, that—

"Great," Todd interrupts again, "so let's share something embarrassing with your readers that'll make the girls jump into bed with me." Todd just won't listen. He never does, at least not to me.

I met Todd at a reading he organized in Denver. That evening, when he talked about the stories he loved, he became so excited that he began to stammer. He has a lot of passion, that Todd, and a lot of energy, and it's obvious that he doesn't really know where to channel it all. We didn't get to talk a lot, but I saw right away that he was a smart person and a mensch. Someone you could depend on. Todd is the kind of person you want beside you in a burning house or on a sinking ship. The kind of guy you know won't jump into a lifeboat and leave you behind.

But at the moment, we're not in a burning house or on a sinking ship, we're just drinking organic soy milk lattes in a funky natural café in Williamsburg. And that makes me a little sad. Because if there were something burning or sinking in the area, I could remind myself why I like him, but when Todd starts hammering away at me to write him a story, he's hard to stomach.

"Title the story 'Todd the Man,'" he tells me. "Or even just 'Todd.' You know what? Just 'Todd' is better. That way, girls who read it are less likely to figure out where it's heading, and then, at the end, when it comes—bam! They won't know what hit them. All of a sudden, they'll look at me differently. All of a sudden, they'll feel their pulse start to pound in their temples, and they'll swallow and say, 'Tell me, Todd, do you happen to live close by?' or 'Stop, don't look at me like that,' but in a tone that actually says the opposite: 'Please, please, keep looking at me like that,' and I'll look at them and then it'll happen, as if spontaneously, as if it has nothing to do with the story you wrote. That's it. That's the kind of story I want you to write for me. Understand?"

And I say, "Todd, I haven't seen you in a year. Tell me what's happening with you, what's new. Ask me how I'm doing, ask how my kid is."

"Nothing's happening with me," he says impatiently, "and I don't need to ask about the kid, I already know everything about him. I heard you on the radio a few days ago. All you did in that crappy interview was talk about him. How he said this and how he said that. The interviewer asks you about writing, about life in Israel, about the Iranian threat, and like a Rottweiler's jaw, you're locked onto quotes from your kid, as if he's some kind of Zen genius."

"He really is very smart," I say defensively. "He has a unique angle on life. Different from us adults."

"Good for him," Todd grumbles. "So, what do you say? Are you writing me the story or not?"

So I'm sitting at the faux-wood plastic desk in the faux-five-star three-star hotel the Israeli consulate has rented for me for two days, trying to write Todd his story. I struggle to find something in my life that's full of the kind of emotion that will make girls jump into Todd's bed. I don't understand, by the way, what Todd's problem is with finding girls himself. He's a nice-looking

guy and pretty charming, the kind that knocks up a pretty waitress from a small-town diner and then takes off. Maybe that's his
problem: he doesn't project loyalty. To women, I mean. Roman-
tically speaking. Because when it comes to burning houses or
sinking ships, as I've already said, you can count on him all the
way. So maybe that's what I should write: a story that will make
girls think that Todd will be loyal. That they'll be able to rely on
him. Or the opposite: a story that will make it clear to all the girls
who read it that loyalty and dependability are overrated. That
you have to go with your heart and not worry about the future.
Go with your heart and find yourself pregnant after Todd is
long gone, organizing a poetry reading on Mars, sponsored by
NASA. And on a live broadcast, five years later, when he dedi-
cates the event to you and Sylvia Plath, you can point to the
screen in your living room and say, "You see that man in the
space suit, Todd Junior? He's your dad."

Maybe I should write a story about that. About a woman
who meets someone like Todd, and he's charming and in favor
of eternal, free love and all the other bullshit that men who
want to fuck the whole world believe. And he gives her a passionate explanation of evolution, of how women are monoga-
mous because they want a male to protect their offspring, and
how men are polygamous because they want to impregnate as
many women as possible, and how there's nothing you can do
about it, it's nature, and it's stronger than any conservative
presidential candidate or *Cosmopolitan* article called "How to
Hold On to Your Husband."

"You have to live in the moment," the guy in the story will say, then he'll sleep with her and break her heart. He'll never act like some shit she can easily drop. He'll act like Todd. Which means that even while he fucks up her life, he'll still be kind and nice and exhaustingly intense, and—yes—poignant too. And that'll make the whole business of breaking it off with him even harder. But in the end, when it happens, she'll realize that the relationship was still worth it. And that's the tricky part: the "It was still worth it" part. Because I can connect to the rest of the scenario like a smartphone to wireless internet, but the "It was still worth it" is more complicated. What could the girl in the story get out of that whole hit-and-run accident with Todd but another sad dent on the bumper of her soul?

"When she woke up in bed, he was already gone," Todd reads aloud from the page, "but his smell lingered. The smell of a child's tears when he throws a tantrum in a toy store . . ."

He stops suddenly and looks at me in disappointment. "What is this shit?" he asks. "My sweat doesn't smell. Fuck, I don't even sweat. I bought a special deodorant that's active twenty-four hours a day, and I don't just spread it on my armpits, but all over my body, and on my hands too, at least twice a day. And the kid . . . that's one hell of a turnoff, man. A girl who reads a story like this—there's no way she'll go with me."

"Read it to the end," I tell him. "It's a good story. When I finished writing it, I cried."

"Good for you," Todd said. "Double good for you. You know the last time I cried? When I fell off my mountain bike and split open my head and needed twenty stitches. That's pain, too, and I didn't have medical insurance, either, so while they were sewing me up, I couldn't even yell and feel sorry for myself like everyone else because I had to think about where I'd get the money. That was the last time I cried. And the fact that you cried, it's touching, really, but it doesn't help solve my girl problems."

"All I'm trying to say is that it's a good story," I tell him, "and that I'm glad I wrote it."

"No one asked you to write a good story," Todd said, getting pissed. "I asked you to write a story that would help me. That would help your friend deal with a real problem. It's like if I asked you to donate blood to save my life and instead you wrote a good story and cried when you read it at my funeral."

"You're not dead," I say. "You're not even dying."

"Yes I am," Todd screams, "I am. I am dying. I'm alone and for me, alone is like fucking dying. Don't you see that? I don't have a blabby kid in kindergarten whose clever remarks I can share with my beautiful wife. I don't. And this story? I didn't sleep all night. I just lay in bed and thought: It's almost here, my writer friend from Israel is about to throw me a lifeline, and I won't be alone anymore. And while I'm taking comfort in that cheering thought, you're sitting and writing a beautiful story."

There's a short pause, at the end of which I tell Todd that I'm sorry. Short pauses bring that out in me. Todd nods and says that I shouldn't sweat it. That he got a little too carried away himself. It's totally his fault. He shouldn't have asked me to do such a dumb thing to begin with, but he was desperate. "I forgot for a minute that you're so tight-assed about writing that you need metaphors and insights and all that. In my imagination, it was much simpler, more fun. Not a masterpiece. Something light. Something that begins with 'My friend Todd asked me to write him a story that'd help him get girls into bed' and ends with some kind of cool postmodern trick. You know, pointless, but not ordinary pointless. Sexy pointless. Mysterious."

"I can do that," I tell him after another short pause. "I can write you one like that, too."

TABULA RASA

For Ehud

SAD COW

A. had a recurring dream. He dreamed it almost every night, but in the morning, when Goodman or one of the instructors woke him and asked if he remembered what he had dreamed, he was always quick to say no. That wasn't because the dream was scary or embarrassing, it was just a stupid dream in which he was standing on top of a grassy hill beside an easel, painting the pastoral landscape in watercolors. The landscape in the dream was breathtaking, and since A. had come to the institution as a baby, the grassy hill was probably an imaginary place he had thought up or a real place he had seen in a picture or short film in one of his classes. The only thing that kept the dream from being completely pleasant was a huge cow with human eyes that was always grazing right next to A.'s easel. There was something infuriating about that cow: the spittle dripping from its mouth, the sad look it gave A., and the black spots on its back, which looked less like spots and more like a map of the world. Every time A. had this dream, it aroused the same feelings in him—calm that turned into frustration that turned into anger that quickly turned into compassion. He never touched the cow in the dream—never—but he always wanted to. He remembered himself searching for a stone or some other weapon; he remembered himself wanting to kill the cow, but in the end, he always took pity on it. He never managed to finish the painting he was working on in the dream. He always woke up too soon, panting and sweating, unable to fall asleep again.

He didn't tell anyone about the dream. He wanted there to be one thing in the world that was his alone. With all those prying instructors around him and all the cameras placed in every corner of the institution, it was almost impossible for an orphan to keep something to himself, and the meadow with the sad cow staring at him was the closest thing to a secret that A. could have. Another reason, just as important, was that he didn't really like Goodman, and hiding the existence of the strange dream from him seemed to be a small but fitting act of revenge.

GOODMAN

Why, of all the people in the world, did A. hate more than anyone else the man who had helped him the most? Why did A. wish that bad things would happen to the person who had taken him under his wing after his parents had abandoned him and who had devoted his life to helping him and others who suffered the same fate? The answer was easy: If there's one thing in the world more annoying than being dependent on someone, it's when that someone constantly reminds you that you are dependent on him. And Goodman was exactly that sort of person: insulting, controlling, patronizing. Every word he said, every gesture he made, carried the clear message—your fate is in my hands, and without me, you all would have died a long time ago.

The orphans in the institution spoke different languages and had little communication with one another, but they shared one essential biographical fact—all of them had been abandoned in the delivery room by their parents when they learned that their newborns had a disease. A genetic disease with a long Latin name. But they all called it "elderness" because it made all the babies born with it age ten times faster than ordinary people. The disease also enabled them to develop and learn much more quickly than ordinary people. As a result, by the age of two, A. had already mastered math, history, and physics at the high school level; knew many classical music pieces by heart; and his paintings and drawings were so adept that, according to Goodman, they could be exhibited in galleries and museums throughout the world.

But, as with all diseases, the advantages paled beside the disadvantages. The orphans knew that most of them would not reach the age of ten, that they would die from illnesses related to old age—cancer, stroke, a variety of heart problems— that their biological clocks would persist in ticking at an insane speed until their worn-out hearts ceased to pump. Over the years, the orphans heard their instructors tell them again and again the same sad stories of their infancy, stories related with the same indifferent tone they used when reading them fairy tales before bed: how their mothers knew at the moment of their birth that their terrible death was racing toward them. And so they chose to abandon them. What parent wanted to bond with a newborn that arrived, like a carton of milk, with such a close expiration date?

At holiday meals, after drinking a bit, Goodman liked to tell the orphans how, as a young obstetrician, he first met a mother who had abandoned her elderness-afflicted baby, how he had adopted him, and within three years, had taught him everything that any other child required at least a dozen years to learn. His tone always emotional, Goodman described how that child had developed right before his eyes at an insane speed reminiscent of the way a plant in time-lapse photography grows, sprouting, developing, blossoming, and withering, all in less than a minute. Goodman would talk about how, at the same time and at an equally rapid pace, his plan was developing to help all those abandoned babies left alone to face the enormous challenges their disease posed. The institution that Goodman founded in Switzerland took in all those sick, brilliant, unwanted children and designed an individual curriculum for each one aimed at preparing them as quickly as possible to go out into the world where they could live their terrifyingly brief lives independently. Every time he told his story, Goodman reached the end with tears in his eyes and the orphans would jump to their feet, applauding and cheering, and A. would stand up and applaud, too, but no sound would emerge from his mouth.

In order for the orphans to go out into the world, they were required by Goodman to pass a life-skills exam. Given once a month, the exam was geared to the particular curriculum of each orphan, and those who received a perfect score went on to a personal interview. According to the rumors, Goodman asked especially difficult questions at the interview; attacked, insulted, and sometimes even struck the interviewees. But if you managed to survive, you could walk out of the institution armed with an identity card, a letter of recommendation that detailed your skills, one thousand Swiss francs, and a train ticket to a nearby city.

NADIA

A. wanted more than anything to leave the institution. More than he wanted to kiss a woman, or hear a divine concerto performed by angels, or paint a perfect painting, A. yearned to pass that exam and the interview that followed it and live out his remaining brief life on a grassy hill under blue skies, among normal people, and not only rapidly aging children and their instructors.

A. failed the monthly life-skills exam nineteen times. During that period, he saw many other orphans leave the institution, some younger than he was and some not half as smart or as determined. But he promised N. that he would pass the next exam in April. N. also studied painting, which meant that A. saw her almost every day, but since A.'s first language was German and N.'s was French, communication between them was somewhat limited. This didn't prevent A. from giving her a small gift every day: an origami seagull he made and painted for her, a real flower he stole from a vase in the dining hall, a drawing of a winged creature that resembled N. soaring above a towering barbed-wire fence.

N. insisted on calling A. by the name she made up for him, Antoine, and he called her Nadia, after a sad, agile Romanian gymnast he had once seen in an old black-and-white film clip. According to the rules of the institution, the orphans were given full names with matching documents only on the day they left the institution. Until then, it was absolutely forbidden to call them by any name or nickname but the identifying letter they were assigned the day they arrived. A. knew that when he and Nadia left the institution, they would receive totally different names and the entire world would call them by those new names, but for him, she would always be Nadia.

THE SECRET DONOR

The agreement between A. and Nadia was simple. It was more a wish than an agreement—they promised each other that they would do everything in their power to pass the exam and the interview, and when they went out into the world, they would live the rest of their lives together.

The institution was funded entirely by donations, and each of the orphans had a personal, secret donor. It was the personal donor who determined the orphan's identifying letter, his future name, his curriculum, and the destination on the train ticket he would receive the day he left the institution. Since Nadia was a French speaker and A. spoke German, they assumed that their train tickets would send them to different cities in Switzerland where they could speak their languages, so they agreed on a plan: The first to reach the train station would carve the name of the destination city on the northernmost bench found there, and upon reaching that city would go to the main entrance of the central train station at exactly seven every morning until they were reunited. But first of all, they both had to pass the exam. Nadia's secret donor wanted her to be a doctor, that was absolutely clear from her personal curriculum. She had failed the anatomy section of her last exam, but she promised A. that this time she would come prepared.

The future that A.'s secret donor wished for him was a bit less clear. Along with his art classes, A.'s personal curriculum placed special emphasis on social and verbal skills, and, among other things, he learned to debate and write carefully reasoned essays. Did A.'s donor want him to grow up to be a leading artist in his field? A lawyer? An essayist or critic? Possibly. In any case, he apparently wanted A. to grow the kind of thick, wild beard suitable to a bohemian, because unlike the other orphans, A. had never received shaving gear, and when he once tried to raise the subject with Goodman, Goodman put an end to the matter with a curt suggestion that A. focus on the upcoming exam instead of "wasting time on nonsense." For his part, A. believed that the donor wanted him to grow a beard because he himself had one. Once he saw Goodman through the gym window talking with an old man who had a long white beard. A. was running laps around the gym and could clearly see Goodman pointing at him and the old man watching him intently and nodding. What could make that old man invest so much of his money on the education of an abandoned child? Kindness? Generosity? The desire to atone for terrible things he had done in his life? And why had he chosen to support a genetically damaged child and not, say, a child prodigy who, with his help, might develop his extraordinary talents and advance all of mankind? A. wondered if he would do something similar for a sick child if he himself were healthy and rich. Maybe there was an alternative universe in which A. was the one standing next to Goodman and pointing at a child, maybe even at Nadia, describing her development, her hobbies, her chances of passing the exam and living the rest of her life in the wild, unprotected world that surrounded them.

THE APRIL EXAM

The time allotted for the written exam was four hours. A. had finished previous exams at the very last minute, and twice he'd had to hand them in without answering all the questions. But this time, he finished twenty-five minutes before the time was up and put down his pen. The instructor asked him if he wanted to hand in his exam, but A. declined. Too much was at stake. He reread his answers painstakingly, corrected punctuation mistakes, and rewrote words he was afraid he hadn't written clearly enough. When time was up, he knew that he was handing in a perfect exam. And, sure enough, among the seven orphans who took the April exam, only he and Nadia went on to the interview.

He saw her as she walked out of her interview with Goodman. She couldn't tell him anything because her personal instructor was right beside her, but her glowing face told him everything. Now all A. had to do was pass the interview with Goodman—and they would both be out of there. Which of them would reach the train station first? Which would be the one to carve his or her destination on the bench? But would there even be a bench? A. was suddenly filled with anxiety. His dream had been not only to leave the institution but to leave it and live with Nadia. What if, because of some tiny hole in their plan, they missed each other? After all, neither of them would know the other's new name, and if neither of them managed to leave their future city, they might never meet again.

"What are you thinking about?" Goodman asked.

"My life. The future waiting for me outside," A. whispered, and immediately added, obsequiously, "and how much I owe this institution, especially you, for bringing me to this moment."

"You sound as if you've finished your business here and you're already waving a white handkerchief at me from the train window," Goodman said, twisting his face into an ugly smile. "As someone who failed the exam nineteen times, that's a bit arrogant on your part, don't you think?"

"This time I passed," A. stammered, "I'm sure of it."

"*You're* sure of it," Goodman interrupted, "but *I*, unfortunately, am a bit less sure."

"This time all the answers were correct," A. persisted.

"Ah," Goodman said patronizingly, "I don't doubt that, either. But an exam is not judged only by the right answers written on the page. Concealed behind the factual answer is intention and character, and with regard to those, I'm afraid you still have much work left to do."

A. stood there, stunned. He searched his feverish brain for an irrefutable claim that would make Goodman change his mind, but the only thing that came out of his mouth was, "I hate you."

"That's fine," Goodman said, nodding, and immediately pressed the intercom button and asked for A.'s personal instructor to come and take him back to his room. "It's good that you hate me. That's part of your development. I don't do what I do to be loved."

"I hate you," A. repeated, feeling the rage rise inside him, "you may think you're a good person, but you're arrogant and evil. Every night before I go to sleep, I close my eyes and imagine myself getting up in the morning and finding out that you're dead."

"That's perfectly all right," Goodman said, "the punishments I give you, the hatred you have for me, they are all part of the process that is supposed to prepare you for a greater purpose. And affection for me or gratitude is not part of that purpose."

THE ESCAPE

It took four security guards to pull A. off Goodman. After the short, violent struggle with them, A. came away with a black eye, a huge bruise on his forehead, and two broken fingers on his left hand, but not only that. He also came away with a security guard's identification tag, which he managed to tear off him as they fought and hide in his pocket without anyone noticing.

That night, A. pretended to be asleep, and at one in the morning, silently climbed out of bed. With the stolen tag, he knew that he could get out of the wing where the orphans were housed. West of that wing was the guest wing, where the orphans were forbidden to enter, and past that was the exit gate. A. had never walked through that gate, but he was sure that the security guard's identification tag would open it for him. And if it didn't, he would climb over it, dig under it, or pass right through it; he would do anything he needed to get out of there.

A. proceeded along the corridor that led to the guest wing and, using the identification tag, opened the heavy iron door. This wing was where the secret donors stayed when they came on periodic visits for updates on their protégés' progress. A. had always pictured that wing as a sort of luxury hotel with a huge dining hall and hanging chandeliers, but now it looked completely different. Its main corridor resembled a corridor in an office building, and every door along it led to a room that looked like a stage set: one looked like a military bunker; another like an elementary school classroom; and the third had a fancy swimming pool with a naked corpse floating in the middle of it.

A. lit his way with an old flashlight he found in the room designed to be a bunker, and focused the light on the corpse's face. It looked like a pulpy mass of flesh and blood now, but A. recognized it immediately: he jumped into the water and embraced Nadia's naked corpse. He was crushed. Devastated. Completely destroyed. This escape was supposed to take him outside to the better life he wanted more than anything, but now, all at once, that desire had been snuffed out. Without Nadia at his side, he had no desire for anything anymore. He heard someone flush a toilet and raised his head. A short, skinny redheaded man in a bathing suit came out of the men's dressing room. He saw A. and immediately began to shout in French, and in seconds, the room filled with security guards. The redhead told them something in a hoarse voice and pointed to A. and the corpse. The guards jumped into the water and tried to separate A. and Nadia, but A. refused to let her go. His last memory was of the strong smell of the chlorine and blood, and then darkness.

ANGER AND VIRTUES

A. woke up tied to a chair. He was in the first room he'd seen in the guest wing, the dusty military bunker where he found the flashlight. Goodman was standing beside him.

"Someone killed N.," he said in a choked voice.

"I know," Goodman said, nodding.

"I think it was a redheaded man, short . . ." A. groaned.

"It's okay," Goodman said, "she belonged to him."

"It's not okay," A. wailed, "she was murdered! You have to call the police . . ."

"In order to be murdered, you first have to be a person," Goodman said in a didactic tone, "and N. wasn't a person."

"How dare you say that? N. was a wonderful person, a good woman . . ."

"N. was a clone. She was a clone of Natalie Loreaux, the wife of the man who ordered her. Philippe, the short man you saw." A. opened his mouth to speak, but air refused to enter his lungs. The room spun, and if he hadn't been tied to his chair, he would certainly have fallen.

"You have nothing to worry about," Goodman said, placing a hand on his shoulder. "The real Nathalie Loreaux is still alive and waiting impatiently for her husband, Philippe, to come back from his short business trip to Switzerland. Now that Philippe has vented his anger on her clone, she will welcome back a much calmer and more loving husband. I can only assume that when Philippe gets home, he'll appreciate Nathalie's virtues a great deal more, and you and I both know that she has quite a few of those."

"But he killed her . . ." A. mumbled.

"No," Goodman corrected, "he destroyed a clone."

"She was a person . . ." A. insisted.

"She *looked* like a person," Goodman corrected him again, "just as you look like a person."

"I *am* a person!" A. shrieked. "I was born with elderness and was abandoned by my . . ."

But the disdainful look in Goodman's eyes kept him from completing his sentence. "Am I a clone, too?" A. asked, tears in his eyes, "Was I ordered by someone close to me who hates me?"

"No," Goodman said with a smile, "with you, it's a bit more complicated."

"Complicated?" A. mumbled, and Goodman took a small mirror out of his pocket and held it in front of A.'s face. In the mirror, A. could see, along with the black eye and some dried blood under his left eyebrow, that his thick beard had been completely shaved off, leaving only a really small, squarish mustache under his nose, and his hair was combed to the side in a strange and ugly way. Now, as he looked into the mirror, A. saw for the first time that he was wearing a brown army uniform. "Your name, my dear A., is Adolf," Goodman said, "and your owner will be here any minute now."

TABULA RASA

The old man with the beard gave A. a scrutinizing look. "You can move closer to him, Mr. Klein," Goodman said. "He's tied up, he can't hurt you."

"I must admit that he really looks like him," the old man whispered in a shaky voice.

"He doesn't just *look* like him," Goodman corrected him, "he *is* him. One hundred percent Adolf Hitler. Not just the body, but also the mind: the same knowledge, the same temperament, the same talents. I want to show you something." Goodman took a small tablet out of his leather bag and placed it in front of the old man. A. couldn't see the screen, but he could hear his own voice coming from the computer. He heard himself scream at Goodman that he hated him and wished he would die.

"Did you see?" Goodman said proudly. "Did you watch his hand movements? Now look at this." A. suddenly heard his voice saying things he had never said, a speech about a strong Germany that would kneel before no one. Goodman stopped the film. "See?" he said to the old man. "They're exactly the same. We took his mind, tabula rasa, and poured everything into it. We've been preparing him for this day from the minute he took his first breath."

Goodman took a gun and a knife from his bag and offered them both to the old man. "I didn't know which you preferred," he said, and shrugged. "Do whatever you want to him. I, with your permission, will wait right outside."

THE FINAL SOLUTION

The old man pointed the gun at A.'s forehead. "I've been waiting my whole life for this moment," he said, "already in the ghetto, when I lost my parents and my brother, I swore to survive and take revenge on the person who murdered my family."

"Shoot," A. urged him, "get it over with. I don't have anything to live for anyway."

"This is not how it's supposed to be," the old man said angrily, "you're supposed to cry now, to beg for your life."

"I'm also supposed to be the man responsible for the extermination of millions and not a clone created in a laboratory who never hurt a living soul," A. replied, smiling crookedly. "I'm sorry, but a person who insists on avenging the dead eighty years after the fact has to make some compromises."

The old man's hand began to shake. "You're Hitler," he cried, "you're a cunning devil who, even now, in your last moments, keeps trying to play tricks . . ."

"I'm Antoine," A. whispered and closed his eyes. He pictured Nadia and himself on the top of that grassy hill, standing in front of matching easels, painting a sunset as red as blood. The metallic click of the gun being cocked sounded so far away now.

CAR CONCENTRATE

———•————————•———

In the middle of my big, empty living room, between the scuffed leather couch and an ancient stereo I still use to play my scratched-up old blues albums, there sits a compressed metal block. It's red with a white stripe running through it. And when the sunlight hits that block at just the right angle, the glare that comes off it honestly dazzles. The thing itself is not a table—despite the countless times I've set stuff on top. And there isn't a person that drops by the house that doesn't ask me about it. Every time, I come back with a different answer, depending on my mood, and depending on who's asking.

Sometimes I say, "It's something from my father." Sometimes, "It's one hefty hunk of memory." And sometimes, "It's a '68 Mustang convertible," or "It's shining red vengeance," or even, "It's the anchor that holds this whole house in place. If it wasn't right there, everything would've floated up into the sky long ago." And then, sometimes, all I say is: "It's art." Men always try to lift it and never succeed. Women mostly touch it tentatively with the back of their hands, as if taking the temperature of a sick kid. And if one of those women goes and touches it with the palm of her hand, if she runs her fingers along the side, and says something like "It's cold" or "That feels nice," I take it as a sign to try and get her in bed.

That people always ask about my block of crumpled steel does me good. It always calms me to know that, in this confusing world of ours, there's at least one thing it's safe to expect. Also it saves me from a lot of other questions, like "So what do you do for a living?" or "How'd you get that gnarly scar under your eye?" or "How old are you, again?"

I work in the cafeteria at Lincoln High School, the scar is from a car accident, and I'm forty-six years old. Not one of those facts is a secret. Nevertheless, I'd much prefer to be asked about my compact and compacted block. Because *through it* I inevitably arrive at any subject I want: from Robert Fucking Kennedy—who was murdered in the year that produced the crushed Mustang I keep in my living room—to the bullshit that is contemporary art. The block never fails to get me to those topics or to anything in between . . . right on up to how Dad would take me and my brother for a spin in the car whenever he'd show up to visit us at foster care. Or to how it took eight people to load that block into my truck, and how the shocks on the pickup nearly gave way under all that weight. I can also wend my way along that line of inquiry until it reaches my dear departed mother who died when I was a baby because my father was driving drunk in another car, gray in color and less cool all around, a car he straightaway upgraded to a Mustang with the insurance money that came his way. Everything really depends on where I want to turn up. A conversation is like a tunnel dug under the prison floor that you—patiently and painstakingly—scoop out with a spoon. It has one purpose: to get you away from where you are right now. And when you dig yourself a tunnel, there's always a target on the other side: empathy that will lead to a fuck; male bonding that will mix most excellently with a bottle of whiskey; something that will reestablish your great value as a tenant to the landlord who's come to raise the rent. Every tunnel has its own direction, but the spoon—at least in my case—is always the same spoon: a convertible red '68 Mustang with white racing stripes that has been compacted down to the size of a minibar and sits in my living room.

Janet works with me in the cafeteria. She's always at the register, because management trusts her. But even there, she's close enough to the food so that her hair smells like a bowl of minestrone. Janet's a single mom, raising twins on her own. She's a good mom, exactly how I love to imagine how my mother must have been. Sometimes, when I see Janet with her kids, I try to picture what would have happened if, in that crash, forty-five years back, my father was the one who'd died and my mother came out of it alive. What would have come out of me and my brother today? Would we find ourselves in different places, or would I still land in a cafeteria kitchen and would my brother still be locked up in the maximum-security wing of a New Jersey prison? What's for sure is that I wouldn't have a crushed Mustang planted on my living room floor.

Janet may be the first woman to stay over at my place and *not ask* about the red block. After we have sex, I make us iced coffees. And while we're drinking them, I try to insert my crushed-up Mustang into the conversation. I start out by resting my cup of coffee—brimming over with ice cubes—on the car. I wait for her to ask. When that doesn't work, I try to ease her there by way of a story. I hesitate a little, wondering which story to tell. I could go with the one about how, when I first got the block home, it stank, and how I started to suspect that they'd somehow crushed up a dead cat inside. Or there's the one where a couple of thieves break into the house and, finding nothing worth anything, try to make off with the cube. Apparently one of them really digs in there trying to lift it. And from the extremes of exertion, he herniates a disc in his spine. In the end, I settle on the story of my father. Something less funny and more personal. I tell her how I searched for him across all of Ohio, and how right when I discover he's dead—and would you expect it to turn out any different—his last girlfriend mentions the car to me exactly as they're towing it to the scrapyard. I tell her how I show up there five minutes too late, and because of that, the sole possession I inherit from my father is not a breathtaking classic car but the hunk of crumpled steel now in my living room.

"Did you love him?" Janet asks. She dips her finger in the

iced coffee and licks it. Something about how she does that, I don't know why, disgusts me. That's what I'm thinking while I'm trying to dodge having to answer. I honestly don't have a lot of feelings in regard to my father—and the few that I do have are uniformly negative. And wrestling with my father issues while we're sipping iced coffees buck naked in the living room is as much of a turnoff as it sounds. But instead of answering, I propose that next time she comes to crash at my place for the weekend she should bring the twins along. "Are you sure?" she asks. Janet lives with her mother, and it's no big deal to leave the kids with her mom and come on her own. "Absolutely," I tell her, "it'll be fun." She doesn't show it, but I can feel that she's happy. And instead of talking about all the shit from my father that my brother and I had to eat before Dad did us a favor and disappeared from our lives, Janet and I fuck right there in the living room while she's leaning on the crushed Mustang and I'm behind. The smarter choice.

The twins are named David and Jonathan. Their father named them that. He thought the biblical reference was funny. Janet wasn't too keen on the idea. It sounded a little gay to her, she says, but she gave in without a fight. After running around with them in her belly for nine months she thought it was nice to concede on that front, to give their baby daddy the feeling that the boys were also a little bit his. Not that it helped. It's been more than five years since she last heard from him.

They're seven years old now and total sweetie pies. As soon as they arrive, they're checking out the yard and they discover the crooked tree. They try to climb it and fall. Try and fall. They get all bruised and scratched up but don't cry even once. I love kids who don't cry. I was also like that. Afterward we play a little Frisbee in the yard, and Janet says that it's hot and that it'd be better if we all go into the living room and drink something. I make us lemonade and set out the glasses on the Mustang. The twins say thanks before they take a sip. You can see that they're well raised. David asks me about the Mustang and I tell him it's car concentrate that I keep handy in case of emergency, you know, in case my pickup breaks down. "And what will you do then?" David asks, his giant brown eyes open their widest. "I'll mix the Mustang concentrate with enough water, wait until it's ready, and then I'll drive it to work." "And it won't be wet?" inquires Jonathan, who's listening to the conversation. "A little," I say, "but still, better a wet car than going by foot."

At night I tell them a story before they go to bed. Janet forgot to bring their books with her, so I make up a story on the spot. It's a story about a pair of twins who, individually, are totally regular. But when they touch each other, they get superpowers. The boys love it. Kids are just crazy for superpowers. After they fall asleep, Janet and I smoke something that Ross, the school janitor, sold her. It's quality stuff. We, the two of us, are floating. All night, we're just fucking and laughing, laughing and fucking.

Only at noon do we wake up. To be more exact, Janet wakes up. And I wake up only from her screaming. I go downstairs to find the whole living room just swamped. David and Jonathan are standing next to the Mustang with the hose dragged in from the garden. Janet is yelling at them to turn off the water, and David immediately runs out into the yard. Jonathan sees me next to the stairs and says, "It's busted. We used a ton of water but it wouldn't mix." The little rug in the living room is totally adrift on this kind of current that's formed, and the old records, too. And I notice my stereo is giving off little bubbles from under the water like a drowning animal. It's just stuff, I tell myself. Just things I don't really need. "This one's fucked up," Jonathan says, still swinging the hose. "They sold you a broken one at the store."

Janet shouldn't have slapped him, and also, what I did on my end, wasn't right. I shouldn't have gotten involved. These aren't my kids, and I definitely didn't need to react the way I did. She's a good mother. It's just finding herself in this very irregular situation that put her under so much pressure. Me, too. And if maybe that slap of hers just slipped out without any evil intent, maybe, you know, she could also try to understand my shove. The last thing I wanted was to hurt her. I was only trying to put a little distance between her and the twins, just until she calmed down. And if there hadn't been all that water sloshing around, she wouldn't have slipped and gotten hurt.

I've already left five messages but she hasn't called back. I know she's completely fine, because her mother told me as much. Only a little blood and a few stitches. They also gave her a tetanus shot because the Mustang's kind of rusty. After she took the twins and left, I worried. So I go to her house and her mother comes out and tells me Janet doesn't want to see me anymore, and after a long smoker's cough, she adds that I shouldn't take it too hard—if I give her enough time and some space, it'll definitely pass.

Tomorrow, when I go to work, I'll bring her a little present: hair gel or socks. She goes nuts for those weird sorts of socks, the ones with big red polka dots or with droopy ears sewn on the sides. If she doesn't want to talk, I'll simply leave the present—all wrapped up nice—next to the register and head into the kitchen. In the end, she'll forgive me. And when I take her home again, I'll tell her the whole story about the car and about my father. About all the things he did to me and my brother. How we hated him. And how when Don went to prison, the one thing he asked was that I find my father and tell him to his face, also for Don, what a shit father he was. I'll tell her about that night at the scrap yard. About how I enjoyed seeing the car he loved so much compacted down to a hunk of crumpled steel, totally stripped of purpose. I'll tell her everything, and then maybe she'll understand. Actually, it'll be almost everything. It'll be everything but how, when I brought my father's car to the scrapyard in Cleveland, the old man's carcass was still warm in the trunk. And after I'm done and Janet forgives me, she'll bring the kids by again. And me and them, we'll close the doors to the living room up tight. We'll shove rags in the empty spaces after we snake through that hose. Then we'll turn on the rusty faucet in the yard until it won't turn any more, and we won't shut if off until that big empty room fills up like a pool.

AT NIGHT

————————

At night, when everyone is asleep, Mom lies awake in bed, eyes closed. Once, when she was a little girl, she wanted to be a scientist. She longed to find a cure for cancer, the common cold, or human sadness. She got excellent grades and had a very neat notebook, and in addition to healing the human race, she wanted to travel to outer space or watch a volcano in action. It's hard to say that something went wrong in her life. She married the man she loved, works in a field that interested her, and gave birth to a sweet little boy. And yet she can't fall asleep. Maybe it's because the man she loves went to pee an hour ago and still hasn't come back to bed.

At night, when everyone is asleep, Dad walks barefoot to the balcony to smoke a cigarette and add up his debts. He works like a horse. Tries to save. But somehow, everything costs just a little bit more than what he can afford. The neckless man in the café already lent him money once and soon he'll have to start paying him back, but he has no idea how he can do that. When he finishes his cigarette, he hurls the butt from the balcony as if it were a rocket and watches it crash into the sidewalk. It's not nice to dirty the street, that's what he tells his son whenever the kid drops a candy wrapper on the ground. But it's late now, he's very tired, and the only thing on his mind is money.

At night, when everyone is asleep, the boy dreams exhausting dreams about a piece of newspaper that sticks to his shoe and won't come off. Mom once told him that dreams are the way our brains tells itself things, but the boy's brain doesn't speak clearly. Even though that annoying dream recurs every night, smelling of cigarette smoke and wet with stagnant water, the boy doesn't understand what it's trying to say. He tosses and turns in his bed, knowing deep down that at some point, Mom or Dad will come in and cover him. Until then, he hopes that the moment he manages to peel that piece of newspaper off his shoe, if he ever does manage to peel it off, a different dream will come.

At night, when everyone is asleep, the goldfish comes out of the fishbowl and puts on Dad's checked slippers. Then it sits down on the living room couch and zaps on the TV. Its favorites shows are cartoons, nature films, and CNN, but only when there's a terrorist attack or a photogenic disaster. It watches TV without sound so as not to wake anyone. At about four a.m., it goes back to the fishbowl and leaves the damp slippers in the middle of the living room. It doesn't care that Mom will have something to say to Dad about that in the morning. He's just a fish, and if it's not a fishbowl or a TV screen, he couldn't care less.

WINDOWS

The man in the brown suit told him that it's okay if he doesn't remember anything, that the doctors said he just needs to be patient. The man in the suit added that the doctors said it to both of them, and if he doesn't remember that either, it's totally okay, that's how it is after an accident like his. He tried to smile and asked the man in the suit if the doctors told him what his name is. The man in the suit shook his head and said that when they found him on the side of the road, he didn't have any papers on him, but for the time being, his name can be Mickey. "Okay," he said, "I don't have a problem with that. For now, we'll call me Mickey."

The man in the suit pointed to the bare walls of the one-room, windowless apartment. "It's not the most beautiful place in town," he said apologetically, "but it's a great place to recover in. Every time you remember something," he said, pointing to the laptop on the desk, "write it on that so you don't forget it. Memory is like an ocean," the man in the suit added in a pompous tone, "you'll see, things will slowly begin to rise to the surface."

"Thank you," Mickey said, and reached out for a parting handshake. "I really appreciate it. By the way, you didn't tell me your name. Or maybe you did and I forgot." They both gave a short laugh at exactly the same moment, and right after that, the man in the suit shook his hand warmly. "My name's not important, we'll never see each other again anyway. But if you have any problems or you need something, you can just pick up the phone next to your bed and dial zero. Someone will always answer, like in a hotel. Our support center works twenty-four hours."

Then the man in the suit glanced at his watch and said he should go because he had three more patients waiting for housing, and Mickey, who suddenly didn't want the man to go and leave him alone, said, "It's really depressing that there aren't any windows here," and the man in the suit slapped his forehead and said, "Wow, how could I forget."

"That's my line," Mickey said, and the man in the suit gave another one of his short laughs as he went over to the laptop and tapped a few keys. The instant he finished, large, brightly lit windows appeared on two of the walls, and a half-open door appeared on the third. Through it, he could see a spacious, elegantly appointed kitchen with a small table set for two. "You're not the first to complain about the rooms," the man in the suit admitted, "and in response, the company I work for has created this innovative application, which affords a sense of open space. From this window"—he pointed to the window that had appeared above the desk—"you can see a yard and an ancient oak tree, and from the other one, you can see the road. It's very quiet, hardly any cars on it. And the door gives a sense of the continuity of a home. It's only an illusion, of course, but the windows and the door are synchronized, and you'll always see the same weather and angle of light in all of them. It's quite brilliant, when you think about it."

"It looks amazing," Mickey admitted. "Completely real. What did you say the name of your company is?"

"I didn't," the man in the suit said with a wink, "and it really doesn't matter. Remember, if anything's wrong or even if you're just in a bad mood, you can simply pick up the receiver and dial zero."

When Mickey wakes up in the middle of the night, he'll try to remember exactly when the man in the suit left the room, but without success. The doctors, according to the man in the suit, said that the memory loss resulting from the blow he received might continue, but as long as it wasn't accompanied by nausea or impaired vision, he needn't worry. Mickey will look out the window and see a full moon illuminating the ancient oak tree. He'll be able to swear that the hooting of an owl came from among its branches. From the window that overlooks the road, he'll see the lights of a truck moving into the distance. He'll close his eyes and try to go back to sleep. One of the things the man in the suit said was that he should sleep a great deal because memories very often return through dreams. When he falls asleep again, he really will dream, but there won't be any solution in his dream, only himself and the man in the suit climbing the ancient oak tree. In the dream, they'll look like children and something will make them laugh, and the man in the brown suit, who'll be wearing denim overalls in the dream, will laugh constantly, a wild kind of laugh, unrestrained, the kind that Mickey has never heard or at least doesn't remember that he's heard. "Look," Mickey will say as he hangs from a branch with one hand and scratches his head with the other, "I'm a monkey, I'm totally a monkey."

Almost a month goes by, at least it felt like a month, and nothing has changed. He couldn't remember anything from the past and continued to forget things that happened only a few minutes earlier. No doctors came to check on him, but he remembered the man in the brown suit saying that there was no need for an on-site doctor's visit because he was being monitored constantly, and that if anything was wrong, the system would react to it immediately. A white van occasionally pulled up next to the oak tree visible from the window, and inside it were a gray-haired, suntanned man and a fat young girl who looked at least twenty years younger than her companion. They groped each other in the van, and once they even got out of it, sat under the tree and drank beer. Nothing changed in the kitchen during all that time. There was a large window there, too, and it let in a great deal of light, but Mickey couldn't see anything through it from his room because of the angle.

He would sit in front of the laptop, stare at the walls for a while, and wait for a memory or a thought to come out of nowhere, like a bird landing on a tree, like the suntanned guy and the fat girl, like . . . At first, Mickey thought he was imagining it: a kind of furtive movement, a shadow without a body that darted across the frame of the half-open door and vanished. Mickey found himself hiding under the bed like a child hiding from night monsters. Now he couldn't see anything, but he heard the sound of a cabinet closing and someone or something flicking a switch. A few moments later, something was visible in the frame of the half-closed door again, moving slowly this time. It was a woman, about thirty. She was wearing a short black skirt and a white button-down blouse, and she was holding a coffee mug with a picture of a sun and the words RISE AND SHINE! encircling it in colorful letters. Mickey didn't come out from under the bed. He remembered what the man in the brown suit had said, and realized that even if he stood up and started waving, the woman in the kitchen apparently wouldn't see him, because the woman didn't actually exist, because it was just a projection on a wall designed to keep him from feeling trapped in his small, windowless room.

The woman in the kitchen was texting on her cell phone now, and as she tapped out the message, her feet tapped nervously on the white marble floor. She had beautiful legs. Mickey tried to remember a girl with legs more beautiful than hers, but except for the girl in the kitchen and the fat girl in the white van, he couldn't remember any girls. The woman in the kitchen finished texting, took a final sip of her coffee, and moved out of Mickey's field of vision. He waited another minute and heard something that might have been the sound of a front door slamming, but he wasn't sure. He hurried over to the desk, picked up the phone, and crouched behind the bed. He dialed zero. A tired male voice answered, "Support Center. How can I help you?"

"In the kitchen . . ." Mickey whispered, "I mean, the projection of the kitchen on the wall . . ."

"In the application?"

"Yes," he continued to whisper, "in the application, there's someone there. Someone lives there." He heard the tired guy type something on the other end of the line. "There's supposed to be a woman there, Natasha, tall, curly black hair . . ."

"Yes, yes," Mickey said, "that's her. It's just that there was no one there before, so it was a surprise . . ."

"Our bad," the tired guy apologized, "we should have informed you in advance. We're always updating and improving the application, and lately we've had more than a few complaints from users that the projected rooms are always empty, which makes them feel lonely. So now we're trying to add a touch of human presence. The Support Center should have informed you of the change. I have no idea why they didn't. I'll add a note to your file and someone will catch hell, I promise you."

"Never mind," Mickey said, "really. No one needs to catch

hell. Everything's fine. Who knows, maybe they did inform me and I forgot. After all, I'm here because of memory problems."

"Your call," the tired guy said. "In any case, I apologize on behalf of the Support Center. It's supposed to be an upgrade, not something that frightens the users. And I must tell you that for now, the service is free, but the company reserves the right to demand additional payment for human presence in the future."

"Payment?" Mickey asked.

"No one is saying that we will," the tired guy said in a defensive tone, "but we reserve the right. You know, it involves additional outlays and . . ."

"Of course," Mickey interrupted him, "it's perfectly understandable. Photographing empty rooms costs next to nothing, but a live person . . ."

"You're pretty sharp," the tired guy said, waking up. "It's a complicated business, especially an application like ours where every system is matched up with a different human figure. At any rate, if it bothers you, don't hesitate to call us at any time. She can disappear just as suddenly as she appeared."

From the minute Natasha appeared, time began moving faster for Mickey. Or slower, actually, depending on the time of day. In the morning, he'd wake up a little before she did and wait to see her drink her coffee, and sometimes she'd even eat some toast or cereal, and text or talk to someone, apparently her sister, on the cell phone. Then she'd go to work, and time would start to drag. Mickey tried to remember things, sometimes he did a few drawings or, more precisely, scribbled in pencil on the lined pages of the notebook he found in one of the drawers. Sometimes he'd read something in one of the travel magazines he found in the bedside cabinet. Once there was even an accident on the road projected on one of the walls. A motorcycle driver skidded and had to be taken away in an ambulance. The suntanned man and the fat girl arrived every now and then, groped each other in the van under the tree, and drove away. But most of the time, Mickey found himself sitting and waiting for Natasha to come back. In the evening, she'd come home and eat a little meal, always simple things—it looked like she didn't really like to cook. She often ate dinner after her shower, barefoot and wearing only a T-shirt and underpants. Mickey would look at her and try to remember. Maybe he once knew someone like her, not Natasha, a different woman, with straighter hair or less beautiful legs, a woman he'd loved or who'd loved him, a woman who'd kissed him on the lips, who'd gotten down on her knees and put his prick in her mouth like it was the most natural thing in the world . . .

The phone woke him up. He answered, half asleep. It was the Support Center, a bored female voice this time. "Is everything okay?" the voice asked.

"Yes," Mickey replied, "everything's great. It's just that you woke me up."

"I apologize," the voice said, "you're being monitored, and your pulse rate suddenly started to increase, so . . ."

"I was dreaming," Mickey said.

"A bad dream?" the voice asked, sounding momentarily less indifferent. "A nightmare?"

"No," Mickey mumbled, "just the opposite."

"May I ask what the dream was about?" the voice asked.

"Sorry," Mickey said, "it's too personal," and hung up.

The next morning, he thought that maybe he'd made a mistake. That maybe he shouldn't have hung up. They might even be so concerned about him there, at the Support Center, that they'd cancel Natasha. Maybe they'd even cut him off from the application altogether. He didn't know if he should dial zero now and apologize, tell them again that everything was fine, that he was sorry he'd hung up, that he just wasn't expecting a call so late at night, that, actually, he wasn't expecting any call . . .

The half-closed door that led to Natasha's kitchen creaked open. Natasha was standing in the doorway, wearing a terry cloth robe, her hair soaking wet. She walked into Mickey's room with her coffee mug in her hand. "I thought I heard you," she said, and gave Mickey a wet kiss on the neck. "Here, I made you coffee." Mickey nodded, didn't know what to say. He drank the coffee. Without milk. One and a half teaspoons of sugar. Just the way he liked it. Natasha put a hand under his blanket and touched the tip of his erection. Mickey's hand shook and the boiling coffee spilled onto his hand and the blanket. Natasha ran into the kitchen and came back with a bag of frozen peas. "Sorry," she said, and put the bag on the back of his hand.

"There's nothing to be sorry about," Mickey said, "it's actually kind of nice."

"The burn?" Natasha asked with a smile. "Because if so, I can tie you to the bed when I come back from work, put on my leather outfit and . . . Just kidding." She gave him another wet kiss, this time on the mouth, checked the burned hand, glanced at her cell phone, and said that she had to run. "I finish at six," she said, "will you be here?" Mickey nodded. As soon as he heard the front door slam, he jumped out of bed and tried to walk through the door to the kitchen. There was nothing there, just a wall with a picture of a door projected on it, a door that now, unlike the previous weeks, was wide open. The painful burn on his hand and the mug with the yellow sun and RISE AND SHINE! printed on it were still there, clear proof that everything he thought had happened here a few minutes earlier had really happened.

He dialed zero. The voice that answered him was familiar. It was the tired guy, even though he actually sounded lively now. "Mickey," the tired guy said as if talking to an old friend, "is everything okay? It says here that last night, your pulse was rapid."

"Everything's great," Mickey said, "it's just that Natasha, you know, from the kitchen in the application, this morning she just . . . I know this sounds a little weird, but she just came into my room, physically came into my room, spoke to me . . ."

"I don't believe it," the tired guy said with real anger. "Don't tell me that they didn't inform you this time, either. No one called you last night to update you on the trial run of our new feature?"

"Some girl did call," Mickey said, "but I was sleeping. She might have tried to tell me and I was just out of it."

"I hear you," the tired guy said, "you think it's important not to complain. I respect that. Even though you should know that many times, complaints are not just bellyaching, they help us fine-tune the system. But it's entirely your right. At any rate, they were supposed to let you know yesterday about the new upgrade that enables the 'neighbor' in the application to actually interact with the user, mainly verbally and sometimes physically."

"Physically?" Mickey asked.

"Yes," the tired guy went on, "and that too, for the time being, is completely free of charge. It came from the users. Many of them said that the presence of the 'neighbors' aroused an intense need in them for human interaction. But you must remember that it's merely an expansion of the existing service and that if you feel uncomfortable with it, canceling is not a problem. The 'neighbor' will go back to living in his or her room and everything . . ."

"No, no. That's not necessary, really," Mickey said, "at least for the time being."

"Great," the tired guy said, "I'm glad you're satisfied. We've only just started to run with this these last few days, and so far the feedback we're getting is fantastic. By the way, if you'd like, there's a way to block the sex with the help of an access code. You know, if you feel it's inappropriate or that things are moving too fast or you just . . ."

"Thanks," Mickey said in a voice that tried to sound unemotional, "for the time being, I have no problem with it, but if I do, it's good to know there's an option."

At night, he dreamed about Natasha and when he woke up, she'd be lying beside him in bed. She slept with her mouth open, like a little girl. Mickey didn't know what she was dreaming about. Or if she dreamed. Her whole entrance into his room, into his life, was completely unsettling, but in the most positive sense of the word. He still couldn't remember anything from before, but that bothered him a lot less. In the morning, when Natasha went to work, he would make pencil drawings of the ancient oak tree, and also of the sea, although he couldn't see it from anywhere in his room, but mostly he tried to draw Natasha. He got better at it with time, and when he succeeded in drawing something that looked especially good to him, he would show it to Natasha, who somehow always managed to compliment him and look indifferent all at once. It was a good time. Questions such as what she was, who she was, why she could move around in the projected spaces while he always remained alone in the room, never came up. It was just a lot of warmth. And hugs. And jokes. Just the feeling that he was not alone in the world flooding his entire body.

One night, he woke up and saw that Natasha was lying completely awake beside him, looking intently through the window. Under the oak tree and the almost-full moon, the fat girl was lying on a checked blanket. She was stark naked, and the older man with the gray hair was on top of her. The man was moving his hips quickly, up and down, up and down, his eyes were closed, his thin lips clenched, and spread across his face was the expression of someone who'd just eaten something unpleasant. The fat girl's entire body vibrated. At first she moaned, but the moans quickly turned into sobs. "You think they're enjoying it?" Natasha asked, almost in a whisper. "It doesn't look like they're enjoying it." Mickey shrugged. "You know them?" Natasha asked, still whispering, and Mickey replied that you might say he did, because this wasn't the first time they were groping each other right in front of his window. "It's not a window," Natasha said, laughing, and hugged him tight, "it's a wall."

Later the arguments began, each one about something else. Natasha said he wasn't ambitious, that she was the only one who worked, that they never went out. She'd start out shouting and end up crying, while he mostly shut up. At some point, she started coming home later, and then it became routine. Mickey dialed zero to the Support Center and spoke to a woman with a runny nose. She told him that they'd been receiving many mixed reactions to the latest upgrade. Some users got along with the "neighbors," and some just didn't. Mickey wanted to ask if there were cases where the "neighbors" didn't get along with the users. That, at least, was what he felt with Natasha. But instead, he asked if it was possible, at this stage of his rehabilitation, to let him go out of his room, and when the runny nose asked him why he wanted to know and if there was a problem in his room, he said no, but he thought that if he could go out a little, it would really help his relationship with the neighbor. Runny nose said she'd pass on his request, but her tone was very unconvincing. That night, Natasha didn't come home at all. She didn't show up until the next night and got into his bed wearing the clothes she'd worn to work, and they hugged each other. Her shirt smelled of sweat and cigarettes. "You and I don't get along," she told him. "I think we need a break." After that, they fucked as if nothing had happened, and she kissed him and licked him all over, and that was nice, but it also felt like a good-bye.

When he woke up, she was gone. The wall with the projected window that overlooked the huge oak tree was just a wall again. The second window had also disappeared, and so had the door to Natasha's kitchen. Four walls, no door.

The man in the brown suit thanked Natasha for the mug of coffee. "I apologize for all my annoying questions," he said. "I know we're not talking about an ordinary user experience here, that this is something much more emotional and intimate, but with the help of your feedback, we can improve the service for millions of other users."

"No problem whatsoever," Natasha said with a sour smile, "you can ask me anything."

The man in the suit asked Natasha almost everything: how much did it bother her that the "neighbor" was restricted to only one room; what did she think about the name "Mickey," and in retrospect, would she have preferred to choose a name for him herself; to what extent did the fact that the "neighbor" didn't know that he wasn't real contribute to her excitement; and was his lack of memory and independent relationships crucial in her decision to end the service. When he asked her if what had developed between her and Mickey could be called "genuine intimacy," Natasha found herself tearing up. "He was just like a real person," she said, "not only in how his body felt. His mind was real. And now that I've broken it off, I just don't know what you did to him. I hope you didn't kill him or something. If I knew that I was responsible for something like that, I'd never be able to live with myself."

The man in the suit put his sweaty hand on her arm in an attempt to calm her, then went to the sink and got her a glass of water from the faucet. She drank it down in one long gulp, then tried to breathe deeply. "You have nothing to worry about." He smiled at her. "You can't kill something that was never alive. The most you can do is turn it off, and in the case of the 'neighbors,' I can assure you that we don't even do that. But let's forget the whole 'neighbors' business for a moment," he said, stealing a glance at his watch, "and return to the basic features of the application, the wall projections of windows that look outside and the door that leads to the additional room—did you have reservations about them as well?"

When you're in a dark place, you're supposed to adjust to the darkness after a while, but in Mickey's case, it was almost the opposite. With every passing moment, the room seemed to be getting darker. He felt his way around, bumping into furniture, running his hands along every inch of the bare walls until he was back at the beginning: four walls, no door. His right hand sailed around the wooden surface of the desk until it found the phone. He pressed the receiver to his ear and dialed zero. The only thing he could hear on the other end was a long, endless beep.

TO THE MOON AND BACK

I celebrate the kid's birthday the day after. Always the day after or the day before, never on the actual date. Always the same shit. Why? Because His Honor the Judge decided that the kid has to be with his mommy on his birthday, even if she's a bitch and a liar who fucks every jerk who smiles at her at work. Daddy is less important.

Lidor and I go to the mall together, not for a present—on my last trip, I bought him a remote-control multicopter drone. Eighty-nine dollars in the duty-free shop—eighty-nine!—and they didn't include batteries for the remote in the box. So we're going to the mall to pick up batteries, but I tell Lidor that it's to have some fun. What can I tell him? Not only did Daddy bring his present a day late but he didn't even check to see if there were batteries inside? No way.

The bitch. Yesterday I say to her, let me come to the party, just for ten minutes. To give the kid a kiss, take a shot of him with my cell when he blows out the candles, and then I'll leave. But she starts with the threats and the restraining orders, texts her boyfriend the law clerk while she's on the phone with me— I can actually hear her tapping—and says that if she sees me anywhere near the building she'll make my life hell.

Lidor wants us to fly the drone first and then go to the mall, but there are no batteries in the remote, and I don't want to tell him that, so I say: First, we'll go to the big candy store on the third floor, the one with the SpongeBob SquarePants helium balloons and the lady with the yellow teeth outside who yells, "Come in! Come in! Buy candy for the little boy," and I'll buy him another present there, whatever he wants.

Lidor says: The mall's great, but first the drone. I lie to him, tell him that the mall closes early. Luckily for me, he's still young enough to believe.

Three in the afternoon, and the mall is packed. To be with him for his day-late birthday, I had to take half a day off work. Judging by how mobbed the mall is, I must be the only person in this country who works. But Lidor, what a sweet kid, he laughs all the time, never whines, not even when we have to wait in line forever to get inside.

At the escalator, he wants to go up the down side, for the fun of it, and I go along with him. It's a good workout for both of us. You have to run as fast as you can so you won't be dragged down, have to strain the whole time not to fall on your ass. Just like in life. A hunchbacked old lady who is coming down tries to argue with us, asks why we don't go up the regular way like everyone else. She'll be in her grave in another minute, and this is what bothers her? I don't even answer her.

When we get to the candy store on the third floor, the lady with the yellow teeth isn't there, only a pimple-faced kid, as thin as a chopstick. I say to Lidor, "Pick out whatever you want. But only one thing, okay? And whatever it is, even if it costs a million dollars, Daddy will buy it for you, promise. What does Lidor want?"

The kid is excited, walks around the store like a junkie in a pharmacy, looks at the shelves, picks things up, tries to decide. Meanwhile, I use the time to buy AAA batteries. Pimple Face doesn't ring it up on the register, even though I wave the money in front of him. "What are we waiting for?" I ask.

"For the kid to decide," he says, and pulls a string of gum out of his mouth. "I'll ring them up together." And, before I can say anything, he starts playing with his cell.

"Do them separately, man," I insist, shoving the batteries into the bag with the drone. "Before the kid comes over. It's a surprise." Pimple Face rings them up, and the cash-register drawer springs open with a ding. He doesn't have small bills to make change for me, so he loads me down with coins.

Just then Lidor comes over. "What did you buy, Daddy?"

"Nothing," I say. "Just some gum."

"Where is it?" Lidor asks.

"I swallowed it."

"But it's bad to swallow gum," he says. "It can stick to your stomach."

Pimple Face gives a stupid laugh.

"You want a present or what?" I change the subject. "Come on, pick out something."

"I want that," Lidor says, pointing to the cash register. "So I can play with Yanir and Lyri, like we have a candy store."

"They don't sell the cash register," I say. "Pick out something else."

"I want the cash register," Lidor persists. "Daddy, you promised."

"I said to pick out something that's for sale."

"You're a liar," Lidor yells, and kicks my leg as hard as he can. "Just like Mommy says. You're all talk." The kick hurts, and when something hurts me I get pissed off. But today I manage to control myself. Because I love my son more than anything else in the world, and today's a special day, his birthday. I mean, the day after his birthday. The bitch.

"How much do you want for the cash register?" I ask Pimple Face, as cool as can be.

"What are you, six years old?" he says with a crooked smile. "You know it's not for sale." He says "six years old" as if Lidor were a moron or something, and I realize now that he's trapped me. I have to choose a side—either I'm with him or with Lidor.

"A thousand shekels," I say, and extend my hand. "We shake on it now and I go down to the ATM and come back with the money."

"It's not mine," he says, squirming. "I just work here."

"So whose is it?" I ask. "The lady with the yellow teeth?"

"Yes," he says, nodding. "Tirza."

"So get her on the phone," I say. "Let me talk to her. For a thousand shekels, she can get a new register. A better one."

Lidor looks at me like I'm some kind of a superhero. There's nothing greater than to have your kid look at you that way. It's better than a vacation in Thailand. Better than a blow job. Better than punching someone who has it coming. "Go ahead, call her," I say, and give him a little push. Not because I'm angry. For the kid.

He taps in the number and walks away from us, half whispering into the phone. I follow him wherever he goes, Lidor behind us. He looks happy. He was already happy earlier, when I picked him up, but now he's flying.

"She says no," Pimple Face tells me and shrugs as if the word had come from God.

"Give her to me." I gesture with my hand.

"She says stores don't sell their cash registers," he says. I grab the phone away from him. That makes Lidor laugh. Daddy's making Lidor laugh.

"Tirza," I say. "Hi, this is Gabi, a good customer of yours. You don't recognize the name, but you'd know my face in a second. Listen, I need you to help me out here. A thousand shekels: you not only buy a new register, but I owe you a favor."

"And where the fuck will we ring up the thousand?" Tirza

asks on the other end of the line. She's in a noisy place; I can hardly hear her.

"So you don't ring it up," I say. "What am I, Internal Revenue? A thousand shekels straight into your pocket. Come on, what do you say?"

"Put him on the phone," she says impatiently.

"The kid?" I ask.

"Yes," Tirza says, getting angry. "Put him on."

I hand the phone to Pimple Face. He talks to her for a minute, then ends the call. "She says no," he tells me. "Sorry."

Lidor takes my hand. "Cash register," he says in his most serious voice. "You promised."

"Two thousand," I say to Pimple Face. "Call her and tell her I'll give her two thousand: a thousand now and another thousand tomorrow."

"But—" Pimple Face starts.

"I can't take out more than a thousand at a time," I interrupt him. "I'll bring the other thousand tomorrow morning. Don't worry, I'll leave you my driver's license as a guarantee."

"She told me not to call anymore," he said. "She's sitting shivah for her father. She doesn't want to be disturbed."

"Sorry for your loss," I say, putting a consoling arm around his shoulder. "So think about it. Two thousand is a lot of money. If she finds out later that I offered it and you said no, she'll tear you a new one. Listen to a grown-up: It's not worth getting into trouble over a small thing like this."

I press the bottom of the cash-register drawer and, *bam*, it opens. It's a trick I learned when I worked at that fast-food place, after the army. "Take out the money," I tell him, but he doesn't move, so I collect the money for him and stick it into the front pocket of his jeans.

"Stores don't sell their cash registers," he says.

"Who cares," I say and wink at him. "Trust me, it's a sweet deal. Wait here for me and I'll be back in five minutes with another thousand so the bills in your pocket don't get lonely."

Before he can answer, I take Lidor by the hand and go down to the ATM. Sometimes the machine gives me problems, but today it spits out the thousand in blue two-hundred-shekel bills without arguing.

When we get back, a sweaty fat guy with a mustache is talking to Pimple Face. I know him; he owns the frozen-yogurt stand next door. When Pimple Face sees us come in, he points at me. I wink at him and put the thousand on the counter. "Here," I say. Pimple Face doesn't move. "Come on, take it already! Lighten up!" I pick the bills up and try to shove them into his pocket.

"Leave him alone," Fat Guy says. "He's just a kid."

"I can't," I say. "I promised my son. Today's his birthday."

"Happy Birthday," Fat Guy says, and tousles Lidor's hair without even looking at him. "Want some ice cream, buddy? A present from me—a cup of ice cream with whipped cream and chocolate syrup and gummy bears on top," he says, and the whole time he's talking, his small eyes stay fixed on me.

"I want the cash register," Lidor says, moving away from him and pressing up against me. "Daddy promised."

"What will you do with a cash register?" Fat Guy asks but doesn't wait for an answer. "We have one, too, but only because the income-tax people make us use it. It's not good for anything. It just makes noise. What do you say—let Daddy take you to the computer store on the second floor and buy you a PlayStation instead. For a thousand shekels, you can get the best one, with Kinect and everything."

I don't say anything. I actually like the idea. It'll save me a lot of trouble here, and later, too, with Lilia, when I take him back home. Because the minute Lilia sees the cash register, she'll start carrying on.

"So what do you say?" Fat Guy asks Lidor. "PlayStation's the best. Races, chases, whatever you want."

"Cash register," Lidor says, hugging my legs tightly.

"Look at what an angel he is," I say, and hand the money to Fat Guy. "Help me make him happy on his birthday."

"It's not my store," Fat Guy protests. "I don't even work here. I'm just trying to help—"

"But you're not." I move so close to him that my face almost touches his.

"I have to go back to the store." Fat Guy shrugs and says to Pimple Face, "If he tries anything, call the police," and leaves. A real hero.

I put the thousand shekels on the counter, unplug the register, and start rolling up the cord, and when Lidor sees that, he starts to clap his hands. "I'm calling the cops," Pimple Face says, and picks up his phone. I grab the phone away from him again.

"Why?" I say. "It's his birthday today. Everyone's happy, don't ruin it." Pimple Face looks at his phone, which is in my hand, then at me, and runs out of the store. I put Pimple Face's phone on the counter and pick up the register. "Now we'll leave here fast," I say to Lidor, my voice cheerful, like this is a game. "We'll go back home and show Mommy what you got."

"No," Lidor says, stamping his feet. "First we fly the helicopter and then we go home. You promised."

"Yes," I say in my gentlest voice. "But the cash register is heavy. Daddy can't carry it and fly the helicopter at the same time. Now the register and tomorrow, right after school, we'll go fly the helicopter in the park."

Lidor thinks for a minute. "Now the helicopter," he says, "and tomorrow the cash register." And right then, just in time, Pimple Face comes running back into the store with a security guard.

"What do you think you're doing?" the guard says. He's a short, hairy guy, looks more like a pinscher dog than a security guard.

"Nothing." I give him a wink and put the cash register back in place. "Just trying to make the kid laugh. It's his birthday today."

"Happy Birthday, kid," the guard says to Lidor, as if he couldn't care less. "Many happy returns. But now you and your father have to leave."

"Yes," Lidor says. "We have to go and fly the helicopter."

In the park, Lidor and I play with the multicopter drone. The brochure says that it can fly forty yards high, but after about fifteen yards it can't pick up the signal from the remote, its propeller stops spinning, and it drops. Lidor likes that.

"Who loves Lidor the most in the world?" I ask, and Lidor answers, "Daddy!"

"And how much does Lidor love Daddy?" I ask while the multicopter drone spins around him, and he yells, "A whole bunch!"

"Up to the sky!" I shout. "Up to the moon and back!"

My cell starts vibrating in my pocket, but I ignore it. It must be Lilia. Above us, the drone is getting smaller and smaller. In another second, it'll be out of our field of vision and will fall. Then we'll both start running on the grass and try to catch it, and if Lidor beats me to it again, he'll laugh that killer laugh of his. There's nothing nicer in this stinking world than the sound of a kid laughing.

GOODEED

A rich woman hugged a poor man. It was totally spontaneous. Absolutely unplanned. He went up to her and asked for some money for coffee. There were no homeless people in her own neighborhood, so he caught her completely unprepared. And he wasn't your typical homeless guy, either. Even though he had a supermarket cart and clearly lived on the street, he looked clean and shaven. The rich woman couldn't find any coins in her wallet, only hundred-dollar bills. If she'd found a ten-dollar bill, even a twenty, she would have given it to him without a second thought, but a hundred seemed to her like too much to give, and maybe a little awkward for him to accept, too.

There are clear rules governing the relationship between the homeless and the average person on the street: speak to each other politely; don't look each other in the eye; don't ask for names; and don't give more than twenty dollars. Anything up to twenty is still within the normal range of generosity, but more than that is an attempt to attract attention, to impress, to force the recipient into saying, "Ma'am, you're a wonderful human being," or else to seem ungrateful. The rich woman didn't want to go there but didn't have any coins or small bills, either, so she said to the man with the supermarket cart, "Wait here a minute, okay? I'll just go into the grocery store and break this."

"He won't break it for you," the guy said. "He doesn't break bills for anyone. And he doesn't let you drink water or use the bathroom, either."

"Ah," the woman said. "But should I try anyway?"

"Don't bother," the homeless guy said. "It doesn't matter. You can give me something another time. What did you say your name was?"

The rich woman hadn't mentioned her name, but now she felt she had no choice, so she told him.

"You're a good woman, Dara," the homeless guy said. "You have a good heart. But I'm probably not the first person to tell you that."

"You are the first person to tell me that," Dara said. "I help my older brother a lot. Mainly financially. And my parents, too. My father, that is. My mother I can't help anymore—she's dead. And none of them ever said I have a good heart or even thanked me."

"That's shitty," the poor man said. "It's frustrating. Makes you feel invisible. Or like a slave. An invisible slave. Someone who gets noticed only when she doesn't give people what they expect to get."

The rich woman nodded. She wanted to tell the poor man that she used to love her family so much, that she'd like to love them now, too, but that she didn't seem to have the strength anymore. She wanted to tell him that when she first met her husband he'd said, "No kids," because it was his second marriage and he already had a fourteen-year-old daughter with issues. So they didn't have kids, and that was actually fine, because their life was good without them. Full. But what killed her was that she never even told him that she actually did want children.

The poor man said, "Let's go and sit somewhere. There's a bench on the corner and a take-out coffee place not far from it. The coffee's on me." But the rich woman didn't want coffee and she didn't want to go anywhere that wasn't her house because she knew it was the only place where she could close the door behind her and cry. She didn't want to hurt the homeless guy, though, didn't want him to think she was being condescending. What finally emerged from all the wanting and not wanting was a hug. A surprising hug, a hug that was giving, but also set boundaries. As if she were saying, "I'm with you," and at the same time, "I'm me." It felt good. Then she handed him all the cash in her wallet—seven hundred dollars—without giving the slightest thought to how it might look or whether it broke the rules. They'd already broken them anyway when she told him her name. The man said, "This is too much," and she said, "No, it's exactly the right amount." After he took the money, she gave him another hug and left.

She had planned to take a taxi in order to get home as quickly as possible. But now getting home quickly was no longer a priority; she just wanted to enjoy this special day. Besides, she had no cash left. So she walked all the way home, and every step she took in her red Jimmy Choos felt like strolling on a cloud.

Later, she told her friends about it. About that sensation of doing what you want, of allowing yourself to feel good. Of giving seven hundred dollars to someone who then said, "Thank you, Dara. You made my day, maybe even my week. You're so kind." When was the last time someone had said that to them? They all understood immediately. They wanted to feel something similar. They were tired of making donations at those dreary charity balls their husbands always dragged them to, where they ended up getting a gold pin and a generic thank-you from the mayor or an aging movie star dragged out of mothballs for the occasion. They wanted the look, maybe even the hug—if it felt natural—from a man whose life they'd rescued from the sewer. Or, if not rescued, upgraded significantly. They wanted to see him cry or thank Jesus for sending them to him, as if they were saints and not just very rich women.

Dara took two of her friends to the southern part of the city in her silver Mini Cooper. It wasn't an ideal car for three—Susan had to fold up her long legs to squeeze into the backseat—but they managed. When they found a homeless man, a guy with a dog and without a leg, Susan and Karen argued about which of them would give him the money. It was one of those arguments in which each person insisted on letting the other win. In the end, Karen got out and approached the man, who was sitting next to a cardboard box with VETERAN written on it in black marker, and put twelve hundred dollars into his disposable plastic cup. The man saw how much money it was—maybe not the exact amount, but he recognized the hundred-dollar bills for sure. He didn't say anything, just looked her in the eye for a long moment and nodded a thank-you. That evening, as Karen lay in bed after everyone had already fallen asleep and pictured that nod behind her closed eyes, she felt her entire body quiver. It had been a long time since anyone had looked at her like that.

The next day, they found one for Susan. But it didn't work out so well for her. That is, the man took the money and even said thank you and gave her a toothless smile, but Susan realized immediately that he was an addict who would piss it all away on drugs, and that there had been no real moment between them. Which isn't to say it was a bad experience, either.

They tried it again a few times, and while they never felt the way they had the first time, they still felt good. And the people who received the money felt good, too, or at least better than before. It didn't take long for Karen to come up with the idea for the app.

It was brilliant. It took off. The software processed all the data about the homeless people or beggars that people uploaded into it, and then it would tell you, at any given moment, where to find the neediest person nearest to you. People just ate it up. *Time* magazine interviewed them about it, and all kinds of people wanted to buy the company from them. They refused to sell, but eventually agreed to give it to Mark Zuckerberg— though only if he promised to donate any profits it made and not keep them for himself.

Zuckerberg looked offended when they said that. "You think I'm getting into this for the money?" he asked. "I already have enough money. I'm getting into this to do good." He said it so beautifully that Dara choked up. "This man is special," she thought. It was no accident that he'd gotten where he was. She told him she wanted a minute alone with Karen to discuss it, and before she could get a word out, Karen grabbed her arm and said, "We have to give it to him."

They'd called their app One Good Deed a Day, but Zuckerberg immediately changed the name to GooDeed, which was shorter and much catchier. Within a few months, it became an even bigger hit. Not WhatsApp, but big.

Six years later, right outside the mall, Dara bumped into the man she'd hugged on the street. She and her husband had signed their divorce agreement only a few weeks earlier, but when the man asked her how she was, she said that everything was fine. Part of her wanted to tell him that she and Walter had split up, and that for the first time in her life, she understood what it meant to be alone, but instead she told him about the app. He couldn't believe it. He knew about it, of course, everyone did, but he hadn't made the connection to himself and their first encounter. Before saying good-bye, she took out her wallet and offered him some money.

"I'm not homeless anymore," he said with a smile. "And you have a lot to do with that. After you gave me the money, I took hold of myself, stopped drinking, and now I teach classes at the community center. My aunt died a few years ago and left me a small inheritance. I used it to buy a small apartment not far from here. Hey," he said, waving his hand in front of her face, showing her the gold band on his finger, "I even got married. And guess what? We've just got twin girls."

Dara was still standing there with the bills in her hand.

"I don't need that anymore," he said, half apologetically. "I did back then, but I'm fine now."

"Take it," she pleaded, tears welling up. "Please, take it. For me."

She had a few hundred dollars in her hand—she didn't know exactly how much, she hadn't even counted it—and it wasn't till she began to sob that he took the money.

CRUMB CAKE

For my fiftieth birthday, Mom takes me to Fat Charley's Diner for lunch. I want to order a pancake tower with maple syrup and whipped cream, but Mom asks me to order something healthier. "It's my birthday," I insist, "my fiftieth birthday. Let me order the pancakes. Just this once."

"But I already baked you a cake," Mom grumbles, "a crumb cake, your favorite."

"If you let me eat pancakes, I won't even taste the cake," I promise. After thinking for a minute, she says grudgingly, "I'll let you eat pancakes, and cake too, just this once, only because today's your birthday."

Fat Charley brings me the pancake tower with a lit sparkler on top. He sings "Happy Birthday to You" in a hoarse voice, waiting for Mom to join in, but all she does is shoot the pancake tower an angry glance. So I sing with him instead. "How old are you?" Charley asks. "Fifty," I say. "Fifty years old and still celebrating with your mom?" He gives an appreciative whistle, and goes on, "I envy you, Mrs. Piekov. My daughter is half his age and she hasn't wanted to celebrate her birthday with us for ages. We're too old for her."

"What does your daughter do?" Mom asks without taking her eyes off the pile of pancakes on my plate. "I don't exactly know," Charley admits, "something in high tech."

"My son is fat and unemployed," Mom says in a half whisper, "so don't be so quick to envy me."

"He's not fat," Charley mumbles, trying to smile. Compared with Charley, I'm really not fat. "I'm not unemployed, either," I add, my mouth full of pancakes. "Sweetie," Mom says, "organizing my pills in a box for two dollars a day doesn't qualify as a job."

"Congratulations!" Charley says to me. "Enjoy your meal and congratulations!" and backs slowly away from our table as if retreating from a growling dog. When Mom goes to the restroom, Charley comes back. "I want you to know," he says, "that you're doing a really good deed. By living with your mom and everything. After my father died, my mother lived alone. You should have seen her. She burned out faster than the sparkler on your pancakes. Your mother can gripe till tomorrow, but you're keeping her alive, and that's a good deed right out of the Good Book. 'Honor thy father and thy mother.' How are the pancakes?"

"Fantastic," I say, "too bad I can't come here more often."

"If you're in the neighborhood, you're always welcome to

drop in," Charley says, and winks at me. "I'll be glad to give you more. Free of charge." I don't know what to say, so I just smile and nod. "Really," Charley says, "it would make me happy. My daughter hasn't eaten my pancakes for years, she's always on a diet."

"I'll come," I tell Charley, "I promise!"

"Great," Charley says, nodding, "and I promise not to say a word about it to your mother. Scout's honor."

On the way home, we stop at a 7 Eleven, and Mom says that because it's my birthday, I can choose one thing as a present. I want a bubble-gum-flavored energy drink, but Mom says I've had enough sugar for one day, so I ask her to buy me a lottery ticket. But she says that, on principle, she's against gambling because it teaches people to be passive, and instead of doing something to change their own destiny, all they do is sit on their fat behinds and wait for luck to save them.

"You know what the chances are of winning the lottery?" she asks. "One in a million, even less. Just think about it: We have a better chance of being killed in a car accident on the way home than you do of winning." After a brief silence, she adds, "But if you insist, I'll buy one for you." I insist and she buys it for me. I fold the lottery ticket twice, once along the width and once along the length, and shove it into the small front pocket of my jeans. My dad died in a car accident on the way home a long time ago, when I was still in my mother's womb, so go figure.

At night, I want to watch the basketball game. The Golden

State Warriors are really good this year. That Stephen Curry is so hot on the three-point shots, I've never seen anything like it. He shoots without even looking at the basket, and the balls drop into the hoop one after the other. Mom won't let me. She says she read in *TV Guide* that there's a special about the poorest places in the world on National Geographic. "Can't you skip it for me?" I ask, "after all, today's my birthday." But Mom insists that my birthday started yesterday and ended at sunset, so now it's just a regular day.

While Mom watches the program, I go into the kitchen and organize her pills in the box. She takes more than thirty pills a day. Ten in the morning and twenty-something at night. Pills for blood pressure, cholesterol, her heart, her thyroid. So many pills that just swallowing them all makes you full. Really, I don't think there's a disease in the world she doesn't have. Except for AIDS, maybe. And lupus. After I finish organizing the pills in the box, I sit down next to her on the couch and watch the program with her. They're showing a humpbacked kid who lives in the poorest neighborhood in Calcutta. At night, before he goes to sleep, his parents tie him with a rope so he'll sleep bent over. That way, the narrator explains, his hump will get bigger, and when he grows up, it'll make people feel really sorry for him and give him a strong advantage in the tough competition with other beggars in the city. I'm not someone who cries a lot, but that kid's story is really sad.

"You want me to switch to basketball?" Mom asks in a soft voice, and ruffles my hair. "No," I say, wiping my tears with my sleeve and smiling at her, "this is an interesting program." It really is an interesting program. "I'm sorry I said mean things about you in the diner," she says. "You're a good boy."

"It's okay," I say, and kiss her on the cheek, "it didn't bother me at all."

The next morning, I go to the eye doctor with Mom. He shows her a chart with letters on it and asks her to read them out loud. She shouts the letters she can see and insists on guessing the ones she doesn't, as if a lucky guess will help cure her. The doctor adds another pill to her collection, to be taken once a day, for the glaucoma. After the doctor, we go to Walgreens to buy the new pill, and so I won't forget, I add it to the box in the compartment for the night pills as soon as we get home. Then I change into my tracksuit, take my basketball, and go out to the children's court. I'm not a great player, but if the kids there are young enough, they're sure I'm a god.

A few years ago, I had a run-in with a redheaded mother with tattoos who got stressed because I was playing with her son. The minute she saw me on the court with him, she told me in a really loud voice that I shouldn't dare touch him. I explained to her that, according to the rules of basketball, you're allowed to touch an opponent when you're guarding him, and that she had nothing to worry about, I knew I was bigger and stronger than her cute little son, and anyway, even when I'm guarding, I do it carefully. But instead of listening, she got even angrier. "And don't you dare call my son 'cute,' you pervert," she screamed, and threw her paper cup of coffee right in my face. Luckily for me, the coffee was lukewarm, but still, it stained my clothes.

After that incident, I didn't go back there for a few months, but then the playoffs started, and when you see good games, it makes you want to play, too. At first, I was afraid the redhead with the tattoos would be at the court and would start screaming again, so I asked Mom if we could buy a basket of our own and hang it in the yard. That was the first time I told Mom about what had happened on the basketball court, and she got very quiet, the way she always does when she's really mad. Then she told me to put on my tracksuit and take my basketball, and we left the house.

On the way to the court, she told me that all the parents of the children who play with me there should thank me because there aren't many grown-ups in the world who still have enough gentleness and goodness in them to play like I do with children and teach them things.

"Sweetie," she said, her voice cracking, "when we get to the court, if you see that stupid tattooed monkey again, you tell me, okay?" I nodded, but in my heart, I was praying that the tattooed redhead wouldn't be there, because I knew that even if Mom is old, she could easily smash that woman's head with her cane.

When we reached the court, Mom sat down on a bench and checked out all the other parents like a bodyguard trying to spot an assassin. At first, I had an empty half-court to myself, and just dribbled and shot baskets alone, but very quickly the kids on the other half of the court asked me to join them because they were missing a player. At the end of the game, when I made the winning basket, I looked over at Mom, who was still sitting on the bench, pretending to be reading something on her cell phone, and I knew she'd seen everything and was proud.

When I reach the court, there are no kids there and I just take some lazy shots that miss the basket, but after about fifteen minutes, I get bored. Fat Charley's Diner is barely a five-minute walk away, and when I get there, it's almost empty and Charley is really glad to see me. "Hey, hoop star," he says, "were you playing basketball?" I shrug and tell him that no one was on the court. "It's still early," he says, and winks at me, "but by the time you finish the mountain of pancakes I'm going to make you, there will definitely be a few people there." Charley's pancakes are really fantastic. When I finish eating, I thank him and ask again if he's sure it's okay for me to eat there without paying. "Whenever you want, hoop star," he says. "The pleasure is all mine."

"And you won't tell my mom about the pancakes, right?" I ask him before I leave. "Don't worry," Charley says, laughing and patting his big stomach, "your secret is buried deep in my potbelly."

The big lottery drawing takes place on Saturday nights. Mom reminds me about it right after she takes her pills. "Are you in suspense?" she asks. I shrug. She tells me again that my chance of winning is less than one in a million, and then asks what I would do if I did happen to win. I shrug again and say that I would definitely send some of the money to that hump-backed kid we saw on TV. Mom laughs and says that the film was made more than ten years ago and it's very possible that the humpbacked kid is now a humpbacked grown-up and he's begged so much that he doesn't need favors from anyone. Or maybe he died from one of those diseases those people get because they don't wash their hands.

"Never mind the children from National Geographic," she says, and ruffles my hair the way I like her to, "what would you want for yourself?" I shrug again because I really don't know. "If you win, you'll probably move to a big place of your own and buy a season ticket to sit in the VIP box for all the Warriors games and you'll hire a stupid Filipina to organize my medications instead of you," Mom says, giving me a not very happy smile. I actually like organizing Mom's pills for her; it relaxes me. "I don't like going to games," I say. "Remember when we went to visit Uncle Larry in Oakland and he took me to a game? We stood in line for almost an hour and the ushers at the entrance yelled at everyone who went inside."

"Then no season ticket," Mom says. "So what do you think you'd buy?"

"Maybe a TV for my room," I say, "but a really big one, not like the one we have in the living room."

"Sweetie," Mom laughs, "the first prize is sixty-three million dollars. If you win, you'll have to think of something else besides a large-screen TV."

This is my first time ever watching a lottery draw. There's a kind of transparent machine full of Ping-Pong balls and each ball has a number on it. The woman operating the machine is blond and she smiles nervously the whole time. Mom says that her bust isn't real and you can see right away that she's had Botox injections, because nothing on her forehead moves. Then Mom says she has to go to the bathroom. This year, she's developed a serious problem with her bladder, and that's why she has to go to the bathroom pretty much every half hour. "Good luck, sweetie. If you see that you've won while I'm peeing, give a yell and I'll run out with my underpants down," she says with a laugh, and gives me a kiss before she gets up from the couch. "But don't yell for no reason, you hear me? You remember what the doctor said about my heart."

The blond with the nervous smile presses a button that turns on the machine. I look at her forehead. Mom's right, nothing moves there. The first ball that drops out of the machine has the number 46 on it, which is the number of our house. The second one has the number 30, which is the age Mom was when my dad died and I was born. The third ball has the number 33, which is the number of pills Mom took every day before she got the prescription for the glaucoma pill, and the last ball has the number 1, which is the number of sparklers Charley lit on my pancake tower. It's weird how all the numbers the blond with the frozen forehead chooses are connected to my life and Mom's, and how all those numbers are written on my ticket. I don't even check the two other numbers, I just keep thinking about what could make a woman inject herself with stuff that paralyzes her forehead and how sad it would be if Mom and I had to live in separate houses instead of together.

When Mom comes back to the couch, I'm already watching the sports channel, but she insists that we switch to Fox because it's time for the evening news broadcast. The newscasters talk about a suicide bombing in Pakistan that killed sixty-seven people. They don't mention the name of the city where the bombing happened, and I just hope it isn't Calcutta. Mom explains to me that Calcutta is in India and Pakistan is a different country, even worse than India. "The things that people do to each other," she says as she gets up and starts walking slowly toward the kitchen. Terror attacks on TV always make her hungry. Mom asks if I want her to make scrambled eggs for our dinner and I tell her I'm hungry, but not for eggs. "Want the last slice of the crumb cake I baked you for your birthday?" she calls from the kitchen. "You'll let me eat something sweet even though it's nighttime already?" I ask. Usually she's very strict about things like that. "Today's a special day," she says, "today is the day you didn't win the lottery. You deserve a consolation prize for that."

"Why are you so sure I didn't win?" I ask. "Because I didn't hear you yell like you promised," she says, and laughs. "Even if I screamed, you wouldn't have heard. You're half deaf," I say, smiling back at her. "Half deaf and half dead," Mom says with a nod as she puts the last slice of cake on the table for me. "But tell me the truth, sweetie, do you know anyone else in the whole wide world who can make a crumb cake as delicious as mine?"

DAD WITH MASHED POTATOES

———•———

DAD

Stella, Ella, and I were almost ten years old the day Dad shape-shifted. Mom doesn't like us to say "shape-shifted" and insists that we say "left," but it's not like we came home from school that day and found the house empty. Because there he was, waiting for us in his armchair, glowing in the full whiteness of his glorious rabbithood, and when we bent to pet him behind the ears, he didn't try to run away, he just wrinkled his nose with happiness. Mom immediately said we couldn't keep him because he took shits all over the house, and when Stella tried to break it to her gently that the rabbit was actually Dad, Mom got angry and told her to stop because it was hard enough as it was, and then she started to cry.

Ella and I gave Mom some jasmine tea and almond cookies, because jasmine calms you down and almonds cheer you up, and that afternoon, Mom definitely looked like she needed some cheering up and calming down. After she thanked us and drank her tea, Mom kissed all three of us and said that the night before, when we were asleep, she and Dad had fought, but in whispers so as not to wake us, and afterward, Dad threw a few things in his white backpack and left the house. Mom said that from now on, we were going to have a tough time, so we all had to be strong and help one another, and when she finished talking, there was a long, unpleasant silence. Finally Dad signaled me with his nose to go over and hug her, and when I did, she started to cry again. Ella, frightened by the crying, whispered to me, "But why is she crying? The main thing is that he came back." But Mom's tears kept coming, and the crying turned into angry sobbing. Stella tried to change the subject, saying that maybe the four of us should do something nice together today, like bake a carrot cake, but that just made Mom more upset. "I want that rabbit out of the house today," she said, "do you hear me?" and went to her room to rest.

When Mom woke up from her afternoon nap, we brought her a glass of lemonade we made ourselves, a slice of bread with butter and jam, and one of her migraine pills, because whenever she wakes up, her head hurts. But first we locked Dad in our room, because Stella said that the faces he made when we spoke drove Mom crazy and it would be much easier to persuade her to let him stay if he wasn't around. She also explained to Ella that when we spoke to Mom about him, we shouldn't call him Dad, because Mom was still mad at him, and until she forgave him completely, we needed to pretend that Dad was just a rabbit.

Mom ate the bread, took the pill, drank all the lemonade, then kissed each one of us on the forehead and said she loved us and now that the four of us were alone in the world, we were her only consolation. Ella told her that we weren't alone, that we had a rabbit, and just as we were her consolation, the rabbit was ours, because even if he couldn't do anything, not even boil water for tea or open a jar of jam, he could still rub against our legs, run around us, and let us pet his soft fur whenever we wanted. Mom said we were kind and generous girls, two excellent traits that would help us a lot in life, but the rabbit still had to go. Then she put on her shoes, took the car keys off the shelf near the door, and said she was going into town to get the man from the pet store to help us; and after he trapped Dad, he'd sell him to a family with a big house and yard who would take care of him better than we could. "No family could take care of him better than us," cried Ella, who had always been afraid of the strange man from the pet store. "He'll be sad without us, and we'll be sad without him." But Mom nodded without even listening and said we could watch TV until she came back.

The minute Mom left, Ella and I told Stella that we had to hurry and hide Dad in a place where Mom and the man from the pet store would never find him; but Stella insisted that it would never work because Mom really knew how to look for things and always found them, even when they were really, really lost. "But he's our father," Ella cried, "we can't let them take him away from us."

"I know," Stella said, and licked her top lip the way we

always do when we're stressed. "I think we'll have to run away with him."

So we took out the three-seater bicycle Dad had built for us himself for our ninth birthday, put Dad in the basket he'd attached on the handlebars for our schoolbags, and started pedaling toward the fields. It was a hot day and we forgot to take water with us, but Stella said that we absolutely could not go home. Of the four of us, Dad looked the thirstiest, but also the happiest. He was always the one who most liked going on outings, and Ella begged us to go back and get him some water, but Stella and I insisted that we had to keep going.

Ella was insulted and said that if we didn't turn around she wouldn't help us pedal, and that almost turned into a fight. But all of a sudden, in the middle of a cornfield, Stella saw a faucet and I managed to turn it on, even though it was rusty, and Dad stood on his hind legs and drank tons of water. He got all wet but looked like he didn't care at all. Then Stella gave him an ear of corn, which is Dad's favorite food, and he gobbled it down in an instant. That, of all times, was when Ella started to cry, saying that maybe Mom was right and that rabbit had come into our house for no reason and wasn't our father at all. When Ella said that, Dad stopped eating the corn and went over to her. She was sitting in the mud, crying, and Dad put both his soft paws on her and licked her. At first Ella was a little scared, but then she started to laugh because his tongue tickled, and when she laughed, we laughed along with her. "Dad is the only one who knows how to make us laugh this way," Stella said, and even though Ella didn't say anything and her face was still wet with tears, I could see from the way she stroked Dad's fur that she knew Stella was right.

At that moment, behind Ella's back, right next to the path, I saw the corn leaves move. At first, I thought it was the wind, but there was no wind that day. It was someone coming toward us who was moving the leaves. I couldn't see his face, but from the movement, I guessed he was much taller than us, as tall as Mom, maybe even as tall as the man from the pet store, whom I hadn't liked from the first time Mom took us to his shop. The cages there always looked dirty, and except for a glowing purple fish, I never saw a happy-looking animal in his shop. I wanted to tell Stella and Ella that someone was coming, but fear paralyzed me. I knew that if they looked at me, they would realize right away that we were in danger, but they were too busy petting dad.

When the mysterious walker appeared from among the corn stalks, Stella pressed Dad to her chest and Ella and I stood in front of her. Dad's nose quivered and his eyes blinked nervously, and it was clear that he was afraid, too. The walker was a tall, skinny boy with huge teeth and pimples on his face, and he was holding a rabbit, too, but his rabbit was plump and had white spots all over its brown body. The boy with the huge teeth stood there and looked at us without saying a word. Dad squirmed in Stella's arms, as if he knew the plump rabbit from somewhere and wanted to talk to him, or at least sniff him, but Stella held Dad tight so he couldn't jump down. "What do you think you're looking at?" she asked the boy, in her scariest voice.

"I don't know," the boy said, "I just . . . never saw three girls who looked exactly alike."

"And what are you even doing here?" I asked, but in a voice a lot quieter and nicer than Stella's.

"Nothing," the boy with huge teeth said, shrugging. "We were on the way back to my grandma's house when it started to get hot and we remembered that there was a water faucet here."

"*We* remembered?" Ella asked.

"Yes," the boy with the huge teeth smiled and pointed to the head of the plump rabbit he was holding in his arms, "my Dad's a rabbit, too."

ROBBIE

On the morning of his birthday, Robbie got out of bed and discovered, in the living room next to the colorfully wrapped presents, that his dad had turned into a rabbit. He recognized his dad right away from the limp, but Robbie's mom, just like ours, didn't believe him.

Robbie's father was an officer in the army. His job was to defuse bombs. Robbie always thought that it was the most annoying and thankless job, because if you do it right, nothing happens, and if you do it wrong, not only do people say you did a lousy job but you get blown to bits. But Robbie's dad loved his job. A few years ago, he couldn't defuse a mortar shell some kid found in a strawberry field, and when it exploded, Robbie's dad caught a piece of shrapnel in his leg and has been limping ever since. When he got out of the hospital, his commanders wanted to transfer him to another job, but he insisted on staying. "It's not like I have to run after the bombs," he explained to Robbie and his mom, who also wanted him to take a different job. When Robbie's mom tried to convince his dad, saying that the new job would be just as interesting, Robbie's dad smiled and said, "Defusing a bomb is like solving a riddle, and you know there's nothing in the world I love more than solving riddles."

On the morning of Robbie's last birthday, there was no cake and no party; nothing but a fat rabbit with a limp in their back-yard. That whole day, Robbie's mom sat next to the phone, talked to people and cried, and that same evening, the police declared Robbie's dad a missing person. Robbie asked his mom to tell them that his dad had actually turned into a rabbit, but she slapped him, then said she was sorry and hugged him. After the slap, Robbie promised not to say the rabbit was his dad any-more, and in return, she let him raise it in the living room.

"Our mom would never agree to that," Stella said, "she's very stubborn." We were in Robbie's kitchen now. His mom was still at work and his dad was playing with our dad on the small rug near the heater. They sniffed and circled each other happily, and Stella said that, from the way they were playing, you could see that they'd known each other for many years. It was starting to get dark outside, and Ella said that if we wanted to go home, we should leave now while there was still some light, because the lamp on our three-seater bike was broken.

"We can't go home," I explained to Ella. "When Mom sees Dad with us, she'll hand him right over to the man from the pet store, and Dad will have to live in a small cage and then with a family he might not like and . . ."

"Yes," Stella said, "you know that there are people who buy rabbits in pet stores and then eat them with mashed potatoes?"

"Don't believe her," I told Ella, who immediately began to cry. "She's just making it up."

"I am not," Stella insisted, "it really happens."

"I don't want anyone to eat Dad with mashed potatoes," Ella said, still crying.

"You can leave him here and come to visit him whenever you want," Robbie said. "We have a big house, and he and my dad get along great."

MOM

On the way home, Ella cried again and barely pedaled. "I want Dad to live with us at home and not in some other boy's house."

"It's not just any house," I said, trying to console her, "it's a house where he has a rabbit friend to play with."

"Yes," Ella said, still crying, "he'll be happy, but what about us?"

"We'll go visit him every day and bring him lettuce and

parsley," Stella said, "and he'll run around us in circles and lick our feet the way you like."

"But for all that to happen, we have to be smart and stop telling Mom that he's Dad. Promise?"

Mom was waiting at home, worried. I was sure she'd yell at us, but she just cried a little and said she was glad we were back and we were okay, and then she hugged all three of us so hard that it hurt. In the living room, sitting in Dad's chair, was the strange man from the pet shop. Mom said that when she came home and didn't see us, she was very upset, and Alex was really nice. He calmed her down and helped her, and he even made her an egg in the basket. The three of us said we were sorry, and Stella lied and said she met a boy in summer camp who really wanted a pet and we all went to bring him the rabbit. "Ella was supposed to write you a note," Stella said, and Ella nodded and said, "I forgot." We all knew that blaming Ella was the best thing to do because Mom always forgave her.

"It doesn't matter," Mom said, "the important thing is that you came back. For a minute, I thought you'd left me too, and I was all alone in the world." Even though I really wanted to tell her to stop saying that, because Dad never left us, I didn't say anything. Ella went over to Mom, hugged her, and said, "We'll never leave you, Mom." When Mom hugged her back, she added, "And if it's okay with you, we can all go back to the boy's house tomorrow to play with the rabbit."

ARCTIC LIZARD

I changed my will today. That's something I never thought I'd do. I joined Unit 14+ a day after President Trump's famous "Twenty-first Century Alamo" speech, but with all due respect to my flag and country, I did it for Summer. She was always there for me: friend, big sister, bodyguard, mother. And it was clear to both of us that if something bad happened to me on the front, everything I'd managed to get hold of and save up during my service would be hers. But this morning, on my way back to base from the hospital, I changed my will.

And now if I hit an IED in a Kiev alley tomorrow, or find myself in the crosshairs of a sniper on the outskirts of Minsk, it'll all go to Sergeant Baker instead. Summer won't understand, I know that. After all, I enlisted for her, for us. And that Baker, he's a real schmuck. The guy did things to me in basic training that should get him beaten up. Maybe even thrown in prison. But after that night on the raft in the Baltic Sea, I can't just go on like nothing happened. The new will is the only way I could come up with to let that bastard know how much I appreciate what he did for me. I can picture him sitting in his motorized wheelchair at his parents' house in Cleveland, watching internet porn, when he gets the e-mail:

"Sergeant Baker, we have good news and we have bad news. To tell you the truth, the bad news isn't so bad—just that another lance corporal schmo who served under you (remember those days? When you could still use your feet to kick the ass of anyone who got on your nerves?) turned his gear in at the Great Quartermaster in the sky to . . . But the good news—brace yourself, my friend, because it really is good—is that you were named in his will and are now the proud owner of 29 rare master characters and 48 lucky eggs. Twenty-nine masters! Including an Armored Arctic Lizard from a limited edition Marines series. Only someone who was in Bangkok on the day of the Silent Revolution could capture that one. There are six of them in the whole fucking universe. And now one of those six belongs to you!"

I can see him moonwalking his wheelchair in reverse, yelling like a madman. I know soldiers who gave ten years in the most dangerous assholes of the world who would happily trade their phenomenal collections for that goddamn lizard. I've used it in 142 head-to-head battles since I earned it, and I won every single one of them. If Baker knew I'd changed my will, he'd crawl over to my sleeping bag tonight and slit my throat, I swear he would. I can practically hear that shit's roars of joy.

But he deserves it. The guy shattered his spine for me. He could have hesitated, like any other soldier would have, just pussy-footed for one second and then he'd have been around to fire the salute at my funeral. But he didn't.

A few minutes after I send the new will in to HQ, my phone lights up with a message from Summer. My first response is panic: she must have found out. Someone from JAG informed her. I mean, her details are on the will, too. All the money and the benefits are still going to her. Maybe when a soldier changes his will, the beneficiaries are automatically notified? I stare at the screen, petrified. I've been through some scary shit this past year: when our jeep lit up like a shooting star in Lima, or on the snipers' beach in Phuket when Timmy Tight-Ass spurted his brains all over my flak jacket, and in that village near Ankara when the rebels booby-trapped the candy and Jemma and Da-mian blew up like a bonfire. But all that is nothing compared with how scared I am to open Summer's e-mail. Because if she's found out about the will, then I have no reason to go back to San Diego. I have nowhere in the world to go home to. It was a mistake to send that new will in. I could have changed it by hand, given it to a guy in the unit and asked him to deliver it to HQ only if something happened to me, instead of uploading it to their server and risking it being sent all over the world.

I open the e-mail the way you turn over the body of a terror-ist who might be strapped with explosives: slowly and carefully. My hands are so sweaty that the touch screen doesn't respond, but after I wipe them off on my pants, I finally manage to open the message. Summer says she hasn't heard from me in a few days and she's worried. So I start writing back about the injury, about how my sergeant saved my life, how I feel I owe him, I have to pay him back. And about how even though he's old, almost twenty, he's probably more obsessed with Destromon Go than we are. But in the middle of writing I stop, delete everything, and send a different message instead, a shorter one: "Everything's fine. I was a little busy." I sign off with three emojis of beating red hearts and one with a finger held up to a pair of lips, like it's a big secret. Then I add, "I'll tell you when I get back." But she'll never understand. She wasn't there.

They set up the 14+ exactly one year after Trump was elected to his third term. America was still licking its wounds from the war in Mexico. Honestly? No one thought it would be that rough. Our drones pummeled them from the air on the front lines, but there was much less we could do about the terrorist attacks in the malls. The whole country was turned into a battlefield. The jihadis and those stinking Russians hooked up against us and started channeling weapons to the Mexicans like there was no tomorrow. The federal government declared martial law. At first there was a draft, and then, when things got really hairy, they announced a new unit and named it 14+. In theory you had to have parental permission to volunteer for it, but after the big Christmas attack on San Diego, Summer and I were left on our own. I mean, we had a state-appointed guardian and all, but the decision was totally up to us. Summer wouldn't hear of it, but there were online ads running constantly. Unit 14+ soldiers were paid real salaries, five times what Summer made at McDonald's, but that's not what tipped the scales. No, what drove me to the induction center was the special collectors' series they showed in the ads. Limited-edition Destromon Gos, master characters with mega CPs that appeared only in war zones. The US military put them up for forty-eight hours, and the only way to get one was to be someone out in the field, which meant either a marine or a Russian commando or whoever the fuck else was fighting us over there. I told Summer: I'll sign up for one year, I'll send money home every month, and when I get back we'll have the best collection in town, maybe even in the whole fucking state. And I was right—I was so right. Six rare masters from three continents. Six! Before I enlisted, the only place I saw mega-CP masters was on YouTube. And now, if I can get through another ten weeks alive, I'll take them back to Summer and I'm king. But if I die, it's all Baker's. Son of a bitch deserves it, though.

Back on base, the guys in the unit seem happy to see me. Marine Cub hugs me and sobs. His ID says Robby Ramirez, but everyone calls him Marine Cub. His ID also says he's fourteen and a half, but I'll be damned if he isn't twelve and a bit. That little squirt barely reaches my chest, and when we shower you can tell he doesn't have a hair on his body, not even on his armpits or balls. Smooth as a baby's butt. The Cub was there the night Baker jumped between me and the Chechens, and he helped me carry what was left of the Sarge back to the ship afterward. The doctors evacuated me, too, but in the field hospital they realized it wasn't nearly as bad as it looked. Just some shrapnel in my gut. "Happy to see you on your feet, dawg!" the Cub says, trying to hide his tears.

After dinner he and I have a little Destromon Go battle, and that's victory number 143 for my Arctic Lizard. "Have you heard anything from the Sarge?" he asks later, while we freeze our brains up with red slushies from the commissary. "HQ updated us about your condition, but we haven't heard a word about Baker." I tell him everything that happened in the hospital. About how the doctors almost couldn't save him, how he'll never be able to walk again. This is all too much for Cub, and he pulls out his cell and starts showing me his collection. "See that one?" he points to a Destromon Go character that looks like a giant mallet: "I found it on the raft the night you and Baker got hit. It may not be a master but it has a special whack-attack mode. Next time we fight, I'm sending him in and he'll pound your fucking lizard into a chicken-fried steak." An announcement over the loudspeakers orders us to gear up and report for roll call with our weapons. On the way I try to find out from the new platoon sergeant where they're taking us this time, but he's as mute as a corpse. We have so many enemies in this fucking world that it could be anywhere.

Fourteen hours later we're flattening an al-Qaeda base in Sinai. We wipe out Jamil "Nine Lives" al-Mabhouh, al-Qaeda's legendary second-in-command, and his elimination is chalked up to me. At debriefing afterward, the company commander falls all over me like some girl, telling everyone how I came back from an injury straight into the inferno, and how when I found myself inches away from Nine Lives with a weapon jam, I didn't lose my cool and smashed his skull in with my rifle butt. He salutes me in front of the whole platoon and says he'll make sure I get a Congressional Medal. They all stand tensely at attention, the commander tells everyone to cheer for me, and they scream like a gang of lunatics.

But the minute he leaves, everyone rushes at Snotty Sammy. Of all the fighters in the unit, he was the one who found a Fire Camel in Sinai yesterday. Which is an epic character—maybe the strongest in the history of the game. With its famous inferno attack and hump defense, Sammy's Camel could fry my Arctic Lizard in two seconds. We pour buckets of ice water and sand on Sammy like we always do in the 14+ when a guy racks up a rare character, and Sammy, covered with mud, starts blubbering and thanking us. Six months ago he was writing book reports on Tom Sawyer and Huck Finn in some crappy high school in Tuscaloosa. If someone had told him back then that he'd ever have a Fire Camel in his collection, he'd have cracked up laughing.

At night in my tent, I get an Instagram from Summer. The picture shows a giant number 10 made out of M&M's laid out all over her belly. Every Sunday she sends me the number of weeks I have left till discharge, written in something I like: Star Wars figures, gummy bears, those little packets of ketchup.

Instead of sleeping, I think about her and about Baker. I try to picture the way each of them would smile if they won, instead of seeing the other one's face, the one who gets screwed. Ten weeks till I make one person happy. Ten weeks tops, maybe even less.

TO: Sefi.Moreh
FROM: Michael.Warshavski
RE: "Glitch at the Edge of the Galaxy" query

Many people have recommended your escape room and I would like to schedule a visit for my mother and myself this Thursday morning or afternoon. In addition, I would like confirmation that the room is accessible to a disabled woman in a wheelchair, as indicated on your Internet site.

Thank you,
Michael Warshavski

TO: Michael.Warshavski
FROM: Sefi.Moreh
RE: RE: "Glitch at the Edge of the Galaxy" query 📎

Dear Mr. Warshavski,

Thank you for your e-mail. We are happy to hear that previous visitors to our "Glitch at the Edge of the Galaxy" room have recommended it to you. We love our escape room very much and are excited to hear that more and more people share that great love. The room is disabled-accessible, and since it touches on astronomy and physics, the well-known astrophysicist Stephen Hawking visited it during his brief stay in Israel (I am attaching a photo of his visit). Unfortunately, the escape room will be closed this Thursday because of Holocaust Remembrance Day, but we would be happy to welcome you and your mother on any other date.

Sincerely,
Sefi Moreh
Director of the "Glitch at the Edge of the Galaxy"
Escape Room

LADDER

—————•————•—————

A few weeks before Rosh Hashana, Raphael called him in for
a talk.

"So what's happening, Zvi, is everything okay?"

"Yes, more or less."

"Glad to hear it, because the truth is that lately, I've started
worrying."

"Why? Did I do something wrong?"

"Heaven forbid, it's just that recently . . ."

"Yesterday morning I didn't rake with everyone, but I had
permission."

"I know, I know. There are no complaints about your
work."

"So what are the complaints about? Someone in the flock
spoke to you? Amatzia?"

"No one spoke to me. No one has to speak, they just have
to look."

"Look at what? Raphael, if you have something to say, just say it."

"How's your Yiddish, Zvi? You understand *farpishter punim*? It's the face a person makes when he's not happy."

"So my face is the problem?"

"Not your face, Zvi, but what's behind it. All of us here are . . . How can I put it? Content. Not just because we have it good here—you do agree with me, Zvi, that we have it good here."

"So?"

". . . but also because of the alternative. Any way you look at it, everyone who comes here feels lucky. More than lucky. Blessed, that's the word. Simply blessed. To be here with us and not with all the losers in . . . you know where."

"I know," Zvi said. "Did you ever hear me complain?"

"No," Raphael said, taking a deep breath, "never. But I've never heard you laugh, either. I've never seen you smile even once since you got here."

"Okay," Zvi said, forcing a smile now. "You want me to smile more?"

Raphael became serious. "No, I don't want you to smile. I want you to be happy, all the time, truly happy. God knows that you have a lot to be happy about—"

"God is dead," Zvi interrupted him.

"I know," Raphael said, and bit his lower lip. "Not a day goes by when I don't think about Him. But we're still here, and heaven keeps functioning just as it did before. And you, as someone who once worked as . . . What exactly did you work as, Zvi?"

"I was a casualty assistance officer."

"That's in the army?"

"Yes."

"Something medical, right? You treated the wounded?"

"No. My job was to inform families that someone was dead. You know, their husband, a son, a brother."

"Terrible. I had no idea there was a job like that."

"How could you know, Raphael? Were you ever in the army?"

"Right. So you used to go to see the families and tell them that their loved ones were dead, and then you went to stand in line at the bank to pay your mortgage, afraid that you would die, too. I'm guessing you were afraid of death, weren't you?"

"Afraid? I was terrified."

"And now you're here. An angel with no debts, no lines to wait on, nothing to be afraid of. You should be grateful."

"I am grateful."

"You should be relieved."

"I'm relieved. Not right now, but in principle."

"You should be happy."

"I'm trying, Raphael, I'm really trying."

"So it's, like, when you get up in the morning, you don't feel happy?"

Zvi cleared his throat. "I do, I do . . . But it's a limp kind of happiness. Like the elastic on underpants that have been washed too many times."

"I have to say, Zvi, that I've been here quite a long time and I've never come across the expression 'limp happiness.' The way I see it, happiness can't be limp."

"It can, believe me. Limp and faded and worn out. You know that feeling of wanting something so much that your whole body aches and you know that your chances of getting it are really, really small, and you stand in your living room in your boxers, covered in sweat, and try to imagine that moment when your lips will meet the lips of the girl you've always wanted, or your son saying, 'You're the best dad in the world,' or the hospital calling to tell you the biopsy was negative? Did you ever want something that badly, Raphael?"

"No."

"Well, I did. And I miss the feeling. You have no idea how much I miss it."

"We don't force anyone to stay here, Zvi. If you're not happy, we can easily transfer you."

"I don't want to go to hell, Raphael. You know that."

"To the best of my knowledge, those are the only two options, and if you really want to be an angel here, you have to be happy. An angel has to be at peace with himself. Serene, that's the word I'm looking for. Because even if it's not written down anywhere, it's part of the job description. Not that being an angel is a job, it's more like an essence and . . ."

"And about that business of raking clouds . . ."

"What about it?"

"Are there angels who do something else?"

"No, but if you're not interested in raking, that's something we can definitely . . ."

"I'm asking because Gabriel once told us that before our matriarch Sarah became pregnant, he went down to see her and . . ."

"It wasn't just him, there were two others with him."

"And I thought maybe . . . maybe there's a chance that instead of raking, I could do something like that? You know, visit people. Give them messages. I've already told you, I was a casualty assistance officer. I have a lot of experience with interpersonal relations in extreme situations, and I'm sure that meeting people every once in a while would really help me. Not just me, the entire system. In all modesty, I'm really good at it."

"We don't do things like that anymore."

"But Gabriel said it wasn't only with Sarah . . ."

"True, but since God left us, we've stopped it. It was always divine insight that influenced the decision to go down and establish contact with people. After all, even if that sort of encounter is efficient, it can cause damage, and none of us— neither I nor Gabriel nor Ariel—has the necessary insight to make that kind of decision."

"What do you mean, you don't have the insight? You're angels!"

"Ministering angels. Our job was to serve God, not to make decisions."

"But you're all . . ."

"Pure, not geniuses. But we're not stupid, either. And if I may ask, why is all of this so important to you? Do you miss the world of the living?"

"Not the place itself," Zvi said with a sad smile, "just the people."

"I must say"—Raphael gave him a similar smile—"that is something I've never heard before. By the way, you know that it's quite possible they are no longer . . . no longer . . ."

"No longer what?"

"That they have been, you know, annihilated, or have annihilated themselves . . ."

"But I only just got here."

"Do you know how long ago you arrived here?"

"No."

"Neither do I. Time moves in a completely different way here. Angels don't age, and neither do clouds. I'm glad to hear that time has been passing so quickly for you. That's a good sign. But who knows how many human years it's been. One hundred? One thousand? One million? But however long it is, it's definitely long enough for such an unstable and vulnerable species to destroy itself."

"You sound like someone who knows something."

"I sound like someone who knows nothing and admits

it. From the moment God died, people haven't been our concern."

"Okay. So if I understand right, the options are either raking clouds or hell," Zvi said.

"You understand right."

"So I'll go back to raking."

SWEAT

Angels never fail. It's almost impossible to fail when you're a pure soul with no desires or needs. But Zvi couldn't help feeling that he was exactly that: a failed angel. Floating on an ocean of serenity yet missing the pull of the whirlpools and waves. Something was wrong with him, something he couldn't share with any other soul. The problem was his alone, and if he didn't find a way to solve it, he'd end up in hell.

Hell was full of souls who had lived like there was no tomorrow, and only after they died did they realize that they had to pay a price for their sins. He didn't want to be the first to arrive there as pure as the driven snow just because he couldn't manage to find himself some happiness even up here in heaven. Zvi knew he had to find a way to stop missing things.

Angels never dream. The closest thing they have to dreaming is staring into space. And the first thing Zvi had to learn was how to stare into space, not focus on concrete things and avoid the frustrating place where he began to compare his now extinct material life to his present lofty existence. And he also had to smile more. And no fake smiles. Angels aren't capable of faking. He just had to find a smile inside himself.

A lot of time had passed since his conversation with Raphael. He couldn't say exactly how much—there are no clocks in heaven—but it was a lot. And even if his desire to return to the material world hadn't completely disappeared, at least it didn't nag at him. Zvi knew he'd never be a perfect angel but he believed that if he kept working on himself, he'd manage to become a standard one, an angel that didn't worry or bother anyone. And despite all his angelic modesty, he knew that the change was visible. After all, out of the dozens of angels, he was the one Raphael had put in charge of garden tools. That was apparently Raphael's way of telling Zvi that he could see he was on the right path.

As the one in charge of garden tools, Zvi had to get to the shed before all the other angels, load the rakes on the shiny wheelbarrow, and wheel it to the section of clouds scheduled to be raked that day. There were other garden tools in the shed: hammers, pruning shears, even a plowshare, but they really only needed rakes. Zvi's favorite moment of the day was when work ended or, more accurately, the moment right after it. All the other angels relaxed, sinking into the sea of sublime serenity that Zvi never managed to experience completely, while he invested all his energy in collecting the rakes to keep himself from sinking into the familiar melancholy. Working helped, like real medicine. Every time Zvi spotted even a sliver of a thought about his former existence or a shadow of longing in his mind, he hurried to the shed and began to sort and organize the tools.

On one of his restless nights, Zvi discovered the ladder. It was a weird, incomprehensible ladder, a paradox with rungs: short enough to stand in the small shed and long enough to . . . honestly? There was no way to gauge its length in material measures, but if forced to do so, Zvi had to admit that its length was infinite. He asked Gabriel about that ladder, and with angelic patience and in great detail, Gabriel began to tell him the story of Jacob's dream, as if Zvi had never read the Bible. When Gabriel saw that Zvi was getting excited about the story, he introduced him to the angel who had fought with Jacob that night, and even asked him to tell Zvi the story from an eyewitness's vantage point. And the angel did. He told Zvi that it had been the first and last time he went down to the material world and that the hardest thing about it for him had been the way people smelled. Jacob, the angel told Zvi, was very weak physically, at least compared with an angel, but he was supposed to hide that and pretend he was fighting a losing battle to defeat Jacob. Jacob, for his part, struggled and strained and sweated rivers. The smell of Jacob's perspiration was so strong that it almost made the angel pass out, but he completed his mission and, finally, when he returned to heaven the next morning, the first thing he asked of God, who was still alive then, was to never send him again on other missions that involved material creatures. When the angel finished his story, he raised both hands in the air as if to say, That's it, this story has no moral, and

Gabriel, who was sitting with Zvi and listening, burst out laughing. "It's true," he told Zvi, "the smell is what always bothered me, too."

THE SMELL OF FRESH LAUNDRY

That night, curled on a cloud, Zvi dreamed for the first time since arriving in heaven. When Zvi was still a newcomer, Raphael had explained to him that an angel's staring into space can sometimes turn into a dream, and that the dream never has a story, images, or time, only color. But the dream Zvi had that night was of a different kind. In it, he was raking clouds when his rake suddenly banged into something hard. Zvi dug in the cloud with his hands and found a metal box that had a picture of butter cookies on it. But when Zvi opened it, he found a small man, a mini-man, inside, and instead of speaking, the little man attacked Zvi in a fury. In the dream, the man was so small and unthreatening that Zvi couldn't understand where he'd found the courage to attack him. At first, Zvi tried to defend himself gently and get the little man off him by holding his shirt carefully with two fingers, but the little man wouldn't back down: he kicked and bit and spit and cursed, and Zvi realized in the dream that the little man wouldn't stop until he destroyed him, that this was a fight to the death. Zvi tried to squeeze the little man between his fingers, to crush him, to tear him to pieces— and couldn't. He didn't know what that tiny, hairy little man was made of, but it was a substance harder than diamond. When

Zvi woke up and found a dewdrop on his forehead, he put it on the tip of his tongue. It was salty.

Zvi got up and went straight to the shed, picked up the ladder, and dangled it from the edge of the cloud. The ladder had an endless number of rungs, and as he descended from one to the other, he tried to imagine the smells waiting for him below: the smell of sweat, of fresh laundry, of rotting wood; the sweet, scorched smell of cake left in the oven too long; the smell of something.

TO: Sefi.Moreh
FROM: Michael.Warshavski
RE: RE: RE: "Glitch at the Edge of the Galaxy" query

Dear Mr. Sefi Moreh,

I am aware of the fact that this Thursday is Holocaust Remembrance Day, and if you will permit me to say, my search for an activity appropriate to that sad and terrible day is exactly why I wrote to you in the first place. I myself see no reason to close your escape room on the aforementioned day. After all, the escape room deals with heavenly bodies, and they, to the best of my knowledge, did not deviate from their orbits when six million Jews were sent to their deaths.

Sincerely,
Michael Warshavski

TO: Michael.Warshavski
FROM: Sefi.Moreh
RE: RE: RE: RE: "Glitch at the Edge of the Galaxy" query

Dear Mr. Warshavski,

Holocaust Remembrance Day is meant to be a day on which we commune with a terrible, traumatic event unlike any the world, and our people in particular, has ever known, and I personally would feel uncomfortable ignoring it and opening our escape room as if it were a normal day. In my humble opinion, it would be better if we all devoted our time—even for only that one day—to deepening our knowledge of that horrendous period, and postponed all other matters, however fascinating they may be, to a less emotionally charged date.

Respectfully,
Sefi Moreh

YAD VASHEM

───

Between the display featuring European Jewry before the rise of Nazism and the one about Kristallnacht, there was a transparent glass partition. This partition had a straightforward symbolic meaning: To the uninitiated, Europe before and after the night of that historic pogrom might have appeared the same, but in truth they were two totally different universes.

Eugene, who was walking briskly, a few steps ahead of the guide, had not noticed either the partition itself or its symbolic meaning. The crash was unsettling and painful. Blood trickled out of his nostrils. Rachel whispered that it didn't look good and maybe they should go back to the hotel, but he just crammed a wad of tissue up each nostril and said it was nothing and that they should just keep going. "If we don't put some ice on it, it's going to get all swollen," Rachel tried again. "Let's go. You don't have to . . ." Then she stopped in mid-sentence, took a breath, and added: "It's *your* nose. If you want us to keep going, we'll keep going."

Eugene and Rachel caught up with the group at the corner, where the Nuremberg Laws were explained. As he listened to the guide, with her thick South African accent, Eugene tried to work out in his mind what Rachel would have said if she had kept going: "You don't have to turn everything into such a drama, Eugene. It's so tedious." Or "You don't have to do it for me, sweetheart. I love you anyway." Or maybe simply, "You don't have to put ice on it, but it'll probably help." Which of those sentences, if any, had she begun to say?

Many thoughts ran through Eugene's head when he first decided to surprise Rachel with two tickets to Israel. He was thinking: Mediterranean. He was thinking: desert. He was thinking: Rachel smiling again. He was thinking: making love in a suite at the hotel as the sun was beginning to set beyond the walls of Jerusalem behind them. And in this entire ocean of thoughts there hadn't been even the slightest thought about nosebleeds or about Rachel starting sentences and not finishing them in a way that always drove him crazy. If he were anywhere else in the universe, he probably would have started to feel sorry for himself, but not here.

The guide was showing them pictures of Jews stripped naked in the snow, at gunpoint. The temperature there, said the guide, was fifteen below zero. A moment after those photos were taken, everyone in the picture—every single one of them, women, the elderly, and children—was forced to get into a pit in the ground and was shot dead. When she finished the sentence, she looked at him for a moment with a vacant stare and said nothing more. Eugene couldn't figure out why she was looking at him, of all people. The first thing that crossed his mind was that he was the only one in the group who wasn't Jewish, but even before that thought had formed fully in his mind he realized it made no sense. "You've got blood on your shirt," the guide said in a detached voice. He looked down at the little spot on his light blue shirt and then up again at a picture of an elderly couple, naked. The woman in the picture was covering her privates with her right hand, trying to retain a bit of dignity. The husband was clutching her left hand in his large palm. How would he and Rachel react if they were ever taken from their cozy Upper West Side apartment, led to the nearby park, and ordered to strip naked and get into a pit? Would they, too, end their lives holding hands? "The blood, sir," the guide said, interrupting his line of thought. "It's still dripping." Eugene crammed the wad of toilet paper deeper into his nostril and tried to give her one of those "everything's under control" smiles.

It began beside a very large picture of six women with their heads shaven. To tell the truth, it had begun four weeks earlier, when he threatened to sue her gynecologist. They were sitting together in the elderly doctor's clinic, and in the middle of Eugene's half-menacing rant at the doctor, she said, "Eugene, you're shouting." The look in her eyes was distant and indifferent. It was a look he hadn't seen before. He really must have been talking loudly, because the receptionist entered the clinic room without knocking and asked the doctor if everything was okay. It had started then and only went further downhill as they stood beside the picture of the women with the shaven heads, thousands of miles away from Rachel's doctor's office. The guide told them that women who arrived in Auschwitz pregnant had to abort before they began to show. Because pregnancy in the camp was nothing short of death. In the middle of this explanation, Rachel turned her back to the guide and moved away from the group. The guide watched her move away and then looked at Eugene, who blurted out, almost instinctively, "I'm sorry. We just lost a baby." He said it loud enough for the guide to hear and softly enough for Rachel not to. Rachel kept moving away from the group, but even from a distance, Eugene could detect the tremor running down her back when he spoke.

The most moving and poignant place at Yad Vashem was the Children's Memorial. The ceiling of this underground cavern was studded with countless memorial candles that were trying—not very successfully—to offset the darkness that seemed to work its way everywhere. In the background was a soundtrack reciting the names of children who had died in the Holocaust. The guide said there were so many of them that it took more than a year to read off all the names in succession. The group started to make its way out of the hall, but Rachel didn't budge. Eugene stood beside her, frozen, listening to the names being read off, one by one, in a flat drone. He patted her back through her coat. She didn't react. "I'm sorry," he said. "I shouldn't have said it the way I did, in front of everyone. It's something private. Something that's only our own." "Eugene," Rachel said, and continued staring at the dim lights above her, "we did not lose a baby. I had an abortion. That's not the same thing." "It was a terrible mistake," Eugene said. "You were emotionally vulnerable, and instead of trying to help you, I sunk into my work. I abandoned you." Rachel looked at Eugene. Her eyes looked like the eyes of someone who'd been crying, but there were no tears. "I was fine emotionally," she said. "I had the abortion because I didn't want the child." The voice in the background was saying, "Shoshana Kaufman." Many years earlier, when Eugene was in elementary school, he'd known a chubby little girl by that name. He knew this wasn't the same one, but the picture of her lying dead in the snow flashed before his eyes for a second anyway. "You're saying things now that you don't really mean," he told Rachel. "You're saying them because you're going through a tough time, because you're depressed. Our relationship isn't doing well right now, it's true, and I'm to blame for much of this, but—" "I'm not depressed, Eugene," Rachel interrupted. "I'm just not happy being with you."

Eugene kept silent. They listened to a few more names of dead children, and then Rachel said she was going outside to smoke. The place was so dark that it was hard to make out who was there. Other than an older Japanese woman standing close by, Eugene couldn't see anyone. The first time he found out

Rachel was pregnant was when she told him she'd had an abortion. It made him furious. Furious that she hadn't given them even a minute in which to imagine their baby together. That she hadn't given him the chance to rest his head on her soft stomach and try to listen to what was happening inside. The rage was so overpowering, he remembered, that it frightened him. Rachel told him then that it was the first time she'd seen him cry.

If she'd stayed a few more minutes in that memorial hall, she might have seen him cry a second time. He felt a warm hand on his neck, and when he looked up he saw the older Japanese woman standing right next to him. Despite the darkness and her thick lenses he could see that she was crying, too. "It's awful," she said to Eugene with a heavy accent. "It's awful what people are capable of doing to one another."

TO: Sefi.Moreh
FROM: Michael.Warshavski
RE: RE: RE: RE: RE: "Glitch at the Edge of the Galaxy" query

Dear Mr. Moreh,

Based on your surname, it is difficult to determine what your roots are. (With a surname meaning "teacher," I wonder: Was it Hebraicized from the Ashkenazi "Lehrer" or the Arabic "Moalim"?) In my case, the situation is much simpler. My name is Warshavski because my family came from Warsaw, and my mother is in a wheelchair because the Nazis put her in it. Holocaust Remembrance Days are especially difficult for her. They flood her brain with memories that any human being would be happy to forget. Since my mother likes riddles and astronomy, I hoped that going to your escape room would distract her a bit and ease her pain. But, if I have understood your worldview correctly, Holocaust Remembrance Day, apart from being an enjoyable day off for you and your business partners, is a day on which survivors are forbidden to find respite from their agonizing memories. And so, as Israelis, our role is to jab an insensitive finger into my mother's bleeding Holocaust wound and twist it around a bit, making sure that her scream of pain is perfectly synchronized with the siren that marks our collective mourning on that day.

Wishing you a meaningful Holocaust Day,
Michael Warshavski

TO: Michael.Warshavski
FROM: Sefi.Moreh
RE: RE: RE: RE: RE: RE: "Glitch at the Edge of the Galaxy"
 query

Dear Mr. Warshavski,

I apologize if my words upset your mother or you, and I would like to clarify the facts: According to municipal bylaws, all entertainment centers must close their doors on national mourning days, including Holocaust Remembrance Day and Memorial Day. It was not a judgment call on my part or on that of my partners to close the escape room on that date, but rather our wish to obey the law.

I sincerely hope that your mother finds some solace on such a sad day. We would be glad to see you in our escape room before or after Holocaust Remembrance Day.

Respectfully,
Sefi Moreh

THE BIRTHDAY
OF A FAILED REVOLUTIONARY

Once there was a rich man. A very rich man. Too rich, some said. Many years ago he invented something or stole someone else's invention. It was so long ago that he himself couldn't remember anymore. But his invention was sold to a huge conglomerate for a lot of money, and the man invested all the money in land and water. On the land he bought, he built lots of tiny concrete cubicles, which he sold to people who were hungry for walls and a roof, and he poured the water into bottles and sold them to people who were thirsty. When he finished selling everything at exorbitant prices, he went back to his enormous, beautiful home and thought about what to do with all the money he'd made. Of course, he could have thought about what he'd do with his life, a question no less interesting, but people with that much money are usually too busy to find time for that kind of thinking.

The rich man sat in his huge house and tried to think of more things he could buy for small change and sell for big money, and also about other things that might make him happy. He was lonely and very much in need of things that could make him happy. He wasn't lonely because he wasn't a nice guy. He was a very nice guy, and very popular, too, and lots of people sought out his company. But since he was also sensitive and suspicious, he thought people only wanted to be with him because of his money. And so he chose to stay away from everyone.

The truth is that the man was right. All the people around him, except for one, did like him, but they also sought him out because of the money. They didn't have enough, or they thought they didn't have enough, and at the same time, they thought he had too much. All the people around him (except for one) believed that if he gave them a little bit of his money, he wouldn't miss it, and their lives would improve drastically. And it was that one person who didn't take the slightest interest in the rich man's money and the future it could buy for him who committed suicide.

The rich man lay on his white marble living room floor, feeling sorry for himself. It was a pleasant spring day and the marble floor cooled his body, but this did nothing to keep him from feeling sorry for himself. The man thought, "There must be something in the world that I want, that could make me happy. Something another person might have to spend his whole life trying to acquire but that I could buy without any effort." But nothing came to mind. He had been lying on the floor for four entire days when his cell phone rang. His mother was on the other end, calling to wish him a happy birthday. She was very old and had so few memory cells left in her brain that she could only store the names of her close relatives and a few important dates. The rich man was glad to hear her voice, and just as their conversation ended, the doorbell rang. Standing in the doorway was a delivery boy wearing a motorcycle helmet, holding a bouquet of fragrant flowers with a birthday card attached. Though the person who had sent him the flowers was not at all nice, the flowers themselves were lovely and they made the man even happier. All that happiness triggered an entrepreneurial thought in the man's mind: If a birthday causes such joy, then why settle for only one a year?

The man decided to put a large ad in the paper offering to buy people's birthdays. Of course, not the actual birthday, which can't really be bought, but everything that comes along with it: presents, greetings, parties, etc. The response was amazing. Maybe it was because of the economic depression at the time, or the fact that people didn't think their birthdays were very important or worth very much, but whatever the reason, in less than a week, the rich man found that his diary was almost completely full with scheduled birthdays.

Most birthday sellers were honest. Except for one elderly man who tried secretly to save for himself a few wet kisses and an ugly painting his grandchildren gave him, all the other sellers followed the contract to the letter and sent the rich man all the profits from their birthday without having to be threatened or sued.

And so, the rich man received many friendly calls every day wishing him happiness, and all sorts of children and old women he didn't know sang "Happy Birthday to You" to him over the phone. His e-mail box was always full of birthday greetings, and gift-wrapped presents arrived at his home nonstop. He still had a few holes in his schedule, especially around February, but his people showed him an endless number of Excel charts explaining that it was only a matter of time before those empty dates were filled.

The rich man was happy. One newspaper published an op-ed piece by some bleeding heart who objected to the rich man's purchase of birthdays, calling it unethical, but even that couldn't ruin his great mood. On that day, he celebrated an eighteen-year-old girl's birthday, and all the heartwarming notes from her best friends made him feel that he had an unknown, exciting future before him.

That wonderful time ended on March 1. The rich man was scheduled to celebrate the birthday of an angry widower, but when he woke up that morning, he discovered that he hadn't received a single card or phone call, and felt slightly cheated. Being such a resourceful man, he decided not to let it get him down, but to do something different. The rich man looked at his calendar again and saw that March 1 was the anniversary of the date the only man who didn't want anything from him had committed suicide, and he decided to go to the cemetery. When he reached the grave of his dead friend, he saw that many other people had come to the annual memorial service. They cried and put red flowers on the grave. They hugged one another and talked about how much they missed the man whose death had left a hole in their lives.

The rich man thought, "Maybe there's something here. Dead people can't enjoy all the love showered on them, but I can. Maybe I can buy the anniversary of people's death, too? Not from the people themselves, of course, but from their heirs. That way I can place a bed covered with dark, one-way glass on the grave, lie inside it, and hear people cry and say how much they miss me."

It was an interesting idea, but the rich man didn't live to act on it. He died the next morning, and like many of the events he had recently celebrated, his death was also meant for someone else. His body was found among the torn wrappings of presents he'd received for a birthday he'd purchased from a failed revolutionary. Later, it was discovered that one of the presents had been booby-trapped and sent by a ruthless, tyrannical regime.

Thousands attended the rich man's funeral. All the mourners wanted his money, but they also liked him very much. They eulogized him for hours, sang sad songs, and placed small stones on the open grave. It was so moving that even the young Chinese billionaire who had bought the rights to the funeral from the dead man's legal heirs and watched it all from his dark cubicle at the bottom of the grave shed a tear.

TO: Sefi.Moreh
FROM: Michael.Warshavski
RE: RE: RE: RE: RE: RE: RE: "Glitch at the Edge of the
   Galaxy" query

Dear Mr. Moreh,

In your last e-mail, you speak about obedience and refraining from making a judgment call, two extremely weighty issues for anyone who wishes to delve into the memory of the Holocaust and learn a lesson from it. I can hardly say that I was surprised to discover that helping an old, disabled Jewish woman is less important to you than obeying municipal bylaws. I can only imagine what your position would be if future bylaws demanded, for example, that you hand over my mother and me to those same authorities. It is superfluous to point out that, based on our e-mail correspondence, you do not seem to be the sort of person who would hide a persecuted minority in his attic.

Well done!
Michael Warshavski

ALLERGIES

The dog was actually my idea. We were on our way back from the gynecologist's office. Rakefet was crying, and the cabdriver, who was, for once, a nice guy, dropped us off on the corner of Arlozorov Street, because Ibn Gvirol Street was closed for a demonstration. We started walking home. The street was crowded and humid and people around us were shouting into loudspeakers. A giant scarecrow with the face of the minister of the treasury on it was planted on a traffic island. People were stacking bills around it. Right when we walked past, someone set fire to the bills and the scarecrow began to burn.

"I don't want us to adopt," Rakefet said. "It's hard enough to raise a child of your own. I don't want someone else's." She paused. Around us people were screaming, but she looked only at me, waiting for my answer.

I didn't know what to say. I didn't really have an opinion in the matter, and even if I had, this wouldn't have been the time to give it. I could see how upset she was. "Why don't we go buy a dog tomorrow?" I finally said, just to say something.

The scarecrow was glowing bright red now. I could hear a police or television chopper circling above us.

"We won't buy," Rakefet shouted over the noise. "We'll save a dog. There are plenty of street dogs who need a home."

And that's how we got Seffi.

We picked Seffi up at the Tel Aviv SPCA. He wasn't a puppy, but hadn't finished growing yet. The caretaker said he'd been abused and that nobody wanted him. I tried to find out why, because he was actually a handsome dog, looked like a purebred, but Rakefet didn't really care. When we came up to him, he flinched as if we were going to hurt him. He trembled and howled the whole way home.

But Seffi quickly got used to us. He loved us and he cried whenever one of us left the apartment. If both of us left at the same time, he barked like mad and scratched the door. The first time it happened, we decided to wait downstairs until he stopped, but he never did. After a few attempts we just never left him alone. Rakefet mainly worked from home, anyway, so it wasn't too complicated.

As much as Seffi liked us, he hated everybody else, especially children. After he bit the neighbor's daughter, we always had him wear a leash and a muzzle. The neighbor made a big scene, wrote letters to city hall, and called our landlord, who did not know we had gotten a dog. We received a letter from his lawyer, demanding we move out of the apartment immediately.

It was hard to find another place in our neighborhood, especially one that accepted dogs. So we moved a little south. We found a place on Yona HaNavi Street. A very large, but very dark apartment. Seffi liked it. He couldn't stand the light, and now he had a bigger space to run around in. It was funny. Rakefet and I sat on the sofa and talked or watched television and he ran around us in circles for hours, never getting tired. "If he were a kid, we'd have given him Ritalin ages ago," I once said. I was only joking, but Rakefet answered seriously, saying that we wouldn't have, because Ritalin was invented not for kids but for lazy parents who couldn't handle their children's energy.

In the meantime, Seffi developed a strange allergy. He got a scary red rash all over his body. The vet said he was probably allergic to dog food and suggested we give him fresh meat instead. I asked if the rash could have something to do with the missile attack on Tel Aviv, because although Seffi had no reaction to the booms, he was very nervous when the alarm sounded, and the rash broke out only after that first alarm. But the vet insisted that that had nothing to do with it and suggested again that we give him fresh meat, but only beef, because chicken would be bad for him.

Seffi liked the beef, and the rash disappeared. At this point he began reacting violently toward anyone who came to the apartment. After he bit the supermarket delivery guy, we decided not to have people over anymore. We were very lucky with the delivery guy. Seffi only tore his calf muscle a bit. The guy didn't want to go to the hospital because he was an illegal Eritrean refugee. Rakefet cleaned and dressed his wound and I gave him a thousand shekels in two-hundred-shekel notes and apologized. He tried to smile, said in a heavy accent that he'd be fine, and limped out the door.

Three months later the rash came back. The vet said Seffi's body had grown used to the new food and that we had to make a change again. We tried giving him pork, but he couldn't digest it. The vet recommended camel meat and gave us the number of a Bedouin man who sold it. The Bedouin was suspicious, because he didn't have Ministry of Health permits to sell the meat. He'd make appointments with me on different intersections, always a couple of hours' drive south. I paid him cash and he'd fill my cooler with meat. Seffi loved it. When I cooked the meat, he stood in the kitchen and barked pleadingly at the pot. His barks sounded almost human, like a mother trying to convince her little boy to get off the tree he climbed. It cracked us up.

One day when I took Seffi out for a walk, he attacked the old Russian man from the second floor. He didn't bite him because he had his muzzle on, but he did jump up on him and push him down to his back. The old man got a serious blow to the head and had to be taken to the hospital. He was unconscious when the ambulance arrived. Rakefet told the paramedic he'd stumbled. We became really depressed, knowing that when our neighbor regained consciousness we'd have to move again.

Actually, I was depressed. Rakefet was mainly worried that Seffi would be taken away from us and put down. I tried telling her maybe that was the right thing to do. He was a good dog, but a dangerous one. When I said this, Rakefet started crying and turned cold toward me. She wouldn't let me touch her. Then she said I was only saying that because I wanted to get rid of the dog, because he was giving us a hard time, with his special food, and not being able to have people over or leave him home alone, and that she was disappointed because she thought I was stronger, less selfish than that.

She wouldn't sleep with me for weeks afterward, speaking to me only when she had to. I tried telling her that it had nothing to do with selfishness. I'd happily endure all the difficulties if I thought the situation could be solved, but Seffi was just too strong and scared, and no matter how closely we watched him, he'd continue hurting people. Rakefet asked if I'd have our child put down, too. And when I said that Seffi wasn't a child, he was a dog, and that she had to accept that, we just got into another fight. She cried in the bedroom. Seffi went over and started howling, too, and I couldn't do anything but apologize. Not that it helped.

A month later, the Russian man's son came over and started asking questions. His father had died in the hospital. Not from the blow to the head, but from an infection he caught there. The guy wanted details on what had happened, because he was suing social security. He said there were deep animal scratches on his body, but the emergency service's report said his father had simply stumbled. He wanted to know if there was anything we hadn't told the paramedics.

We didn't let him in the apartment, but as we spoke in the stairwell, Seffi began barking and the guy asked questions about the dog and wanted to see him. We told him he couldn't come in, that the dog was new, we only got him ten days ago, long after his father had the fall. He insisted on seeing him anyway, and when we refused again, he threatened to come back with the police.

That very night we found an apartment for rent in the Florentin neighborhood. It was small and noisy but the landlord didn't mind the dog. Rakefet and I went back to sleeping together. She was still a bit cold, but the drama with the Russian's son had brought us closer together again. She also saw that I was standing up for Seffi, and that softened her.

Then Seffi's rash returned.

Our old vet was no longer available. It turned out he was a high-up in the military and was killed on reserve duty, performing a retaliation attack in Syria. Rakefet refused to try to find a new vet, scared he would tell us to put Seffi down. We didn't want to keep giving him camel meat. We tried fish and meat substitutes instead, but he wouldn't touch anything, and after he didn't eat for two days, Rakefet said we had to find a different kind of meat before he starved to death.

Rakefet crushed some sleeping pills her mother gave her a long time ago when we flew to New York for our honeymoon, and put them in a bowl of milk. From our balcony we saw some cats in the yard approach the bowl and sniff the milk. None of them touched it, except for one thin, red-haired cat. Rakefet told me to go downstairs and follow him, but the cat wasn't going anywhere. He lay down by the bowl. He didn't even move when I approached. He looked at me with the most human eyes, giving me a sad but accepting look, like he knew just what was going to happen and had to go with it because the world was shit. When the cat was completely asleep, I picked him up but couldn't take him upstairs. I felt the skinny cat breathing in my arms and couldn't do it. I sat on the steps, crying. A few minutes later I felt a hand on my shoulder. It was Rakefet. I never even heard her coming down the stairs. "Leave it," she told me. "Leave the cat here and come upstairs. We'll find another way."

We decided to try pigeons. On Washington Avenue, right by our house, there were a ton of fat pigeons that the old neighborhood residents liked to feed. We searched the internet for ways to hunt them. There were plenty, but they all seemed pretty complicated. Finally, I bought a professional marble-shooting slingshot at a military equipment store in the central bus station. After a few days of studying and practicing I was quite the marksman. After Seffi ate one pigeon and seemed to respond well, Rakefet and I drank two bottles of wine and fucked all night long. Happy fucking. We felt very, very good, and we felt that we'd earned all that goodness, fair and square.

Rakefet suggested I hunt the pigeons at dawn, when the streets were empty, to avoid any eyewitnesses. Ever since then, twice a week I set the alarm for four-thirty a.m., go out while the whole street is still asleep, scatter bread crumbs, and hide in the bushes. I'm addicted to these hours, to the gentle, cold air of the morning—not freezing cold, but cold enough to wake you up. I lie in the bushes, listening to music through my earphones. It's my quality time. All alone, just me, my thoughts, my music, and occasionally a pigeon in my sights. First I hunted only two or three at a time, but now I start getting more. It's fun, coming home to my wife with my game like some sort of caveman. It's really improving our relationship, or at least helping us fix whatever broke back when Seffi jumped on the old man.

When we googled hunting methods, Rakefet found a great French pigeon recipe—pigeons in wine, stuffed with rice. It's the most delicious thing in the world, and Seffi loves it when we eat the same food as him. Sometimes, just for kicks, I sit next to him on the kitchen floor and we both howl at Rakefet as she cooks our pigeons.

"Get up," she always says, laughing. "Get up, or I'll think I married a dog."

But I tilt my head back, close my eyes, and keep howling, and I only stop when Seffi comes closer and lovingly licks my face.

TO: Michael.Warshavski
FROM: Sefi.Moreh
RE: RE: RE: RE: RE: RE: RE: RE: "Glitch at the Edge of the Galaxy" query 📎

Dear Michael,

Your last e-mail hurt me deeply. Comparing me to Nazi collaborators was inappropriate. And, regarding the question you raised in one of your previous emails: my grandparents changed their surname from "Moalim" to "Moreh" when they arrived in Israel from Iraq. They left their country because my grandfather, who was a fervent Zionist, was persecuted and tortured. So, despite the fact that my roots are not in eastern Europe, my family also fell victim to persecution and suffering. Out of empathy for your mother's emotional state (and despite the aggressive and hurtful style you chose to write in), I have decided, without consulting with my partners, to host you and your mother in our escape room on the morning of Holocaust Remembrance Day in the hope that attempting to solve the profound riddles and observing the heavenly bodies will help your mother to escape—however briefly—the harsh memories that must certainly haunt her.

Hoping to see you soon,
Sefi Moreh

P.S. I am attaching a photo of my grandfather seated atop an armored vehicle after the liberation of Beit Guvrin.

FUNGUS

The skinny guy fell to the café floor. His stomach hurt more than he thought it ever possibly could. A series of involuntary spasms shook his body. "This is what it must be like when you're going to die," he thought. "But this can't be the end. I'm too young, and it's too embarrassing to die like this, in shorts and Crocs, on the floor of a café that was once trendy but hasn't been making a go of it for years." The guy opened his mouth to scream for help but didn't have enough air in his lungs to let out a scream. This story isn't about him.

The waitress who went over to the skinny guy was named Galia. She never wanted to be a waitress. She'd always dreamed of being a preschool teacher. But there's no money in teaching kids, and there was in waitressing. Not an awful lot, but enough to cover her rent and all. That year, though, she'd started studying special education at Beit Berl College. On the days she was at school, she worked the night shift at the café. Not even a dog came to the café at night, and she earned less than half the tips, but school was important to her. "Are you okay?" she asked the guy on the floor. She knew he wasn't, but she asked anyway, out of embarrassment. This story isn't about her, either.

"I'm dying," the guy said, "I'm dying, call an ambulance."

"There's no point," said a dark-skinned bald guy who had been sitting at the bar reading the financial pages. "It'll take about an hour for the ambulance to get here. They've cut their budget down to the bone. They work Saturday hours all week now." While the man was telling Galia this, he was hauling the skinny guy onto his back, and added, "I'll take him to the ER. My car is parked right outside." He did this because he was a good man—because he was a good man and wanted the waitress to see that. Five months had passed since his divorce, and those few words he'd spoken to Galia were the closest he'd come in that period to having an intimate conversation with a pretty girl. This story isn't about him, either.

Traffic was jammed up all the way to the hospital. The skinny guy, who was lying in the back of the car, moaned in an almost inaudible voice and drooled on the upholstery of the dark-skinned bald guy's new Alfa sports car. When he got divorced, his friends told him that he had to replace his family-sized Mitsubishi with something else, a bachelor's car. Girls learn a lot about you from the car you drive. A Mitsubishi says: Wiped-out divorced guy seeks shrew to take place of last bitch. An Alfa sports car says: A cool guy, young at heart, seeks adventure. That skinny guy convulsing in the backseat was kind of an adventure. The bald guy thought, "I'm like an ambulance now. I don't have a siren but I can beep for other cars to let me pass, go through red lights, like in the movies." While he was thinking all that, he floored the gas pedal. While he was thinking all that, a white Renault van crashed into the side of his Alfa. The driver of the Renault was religious. The driver of the Renault didn't have his seat belt on. The crash killed him on the spot. This story isn't about him, either.

Whose fault was the crash? The dark-skinned bald guy who accelerated and ignored the stop sign? Not really. The van driver who didn't buckle his seat belt and was driving over the speed limit? Not him, either. There's only one person responsible for that accident. Why did I invent all these people? Why did I kill a guy wearing a yarmulke who never did anything to me? Why did I make a nonexistent guy have pain? Why did I destroy a dark-skinned bald guy's family unit? The fact that you invent something doesn't exempt you from responsibility, and unlike life, where you can shrug and point up to God in heaven, there's no excuse here. In a story, you're God. If your protagonist failed, it's only because you made him fail. If something bad happened to him, it's only because you wanted it to. You wanted to watch him wallow in his own blood.

My wife comes in the room and asks, "Are you writing?" She wants to ask me something. Something else. I can see it on her face, but at the same time, she doesn't want to interrupt me.

She doesn't want to, but she already has. I say yes, but never mind. This story isn't working. It's not even a story. It's an itch. It's a fungus under my fingernail, I tell her. She nods as if she understands what I'm talking about. She doesn't. But that doesn't mean she doesn't love me. This story is about us.

TO: Sefi.Moreh
FROM: Michael.Warshavski
RE: RE: RE: RE: RE: RE: RE: RE: RE: "Glitch at the Edge of the Galaxy" query 📎

Thank you, Sefi.

My mother and I greatly appreciate the flexibility and are happy that we will have the privilege of visiting your escape room, whose riddles you speak so highly of. Without entering into a pedantic argument regarding the justice of my claims, the fact that you were offended justifies an apology. Please accept my apology and, at the same time, my reservations about the unseemly comparison between the persecution of your grandfather in Iraq and my mother's suffering. To the best of my knowledge, there was no genocide in Iraq and no Jew was led to the gas chambers or the crematoria (I doubt that, at the time, the Iraqi people had technology advanced enough to build gas chambers). I assume that your idealistic grandfather endured many unpleasant experiences in his homeland, but any comparison between them and the horrors of the Holocaust are an indication of insensitivity and ignorance. I am glad that, this Thursday, we will focus on astronomy and not on the history of our people, thereby avoiding additional discord between us.

Yours,
Michael Warshavski

P.S. Thank you for the photograph. Your grandfather does indeed look like a brave and down-to-earth fellow and I am glad he was able to realize his dream.

Unfortunately, my grandparents, who were sent to Auschwitz, were a bit less fortunate. Since I do not have a picture of them, I am attaching one of the arch-murderer (who was never caught and tried) responsible for their deaths.

CHIPS

———————

The first girl I ever kissed on the mouth was named Vered, which is also the name of a flower in Hebrew. It was a long kiss. If it had been up to me, it would have gone on forever, or at least until we got old and shriveled and died, but Vered stopped it first. We were both quiet for a minute, and then I said thank you. She said, "You're totally fucked up." And after another short silence, she added, "That thank-you is such a turnoff, you know? We kissed, the two of us, it's not like I'm some old aunt who brought you a present for the holiday." And I said, "Don't be mad, it was just a thank-you." And she said, "Shut up, okay?" So I shut up. I didn't want to piss off the first girl who ever kissed me. I just wanted to make her feel happy, but I didn't know how. She didn't say anything further, just looked at me a little, and then unbuckled my belt and started to blow me. Just like that, out of the blue, in the middle of the hall in her parents' apartment. They were out. I still kept my mouth shut. I already knew that I didn't know how to act at times like this, so I tried to do as little as possible.

After she blew me, we fucked on the plastic-covered living room couch. After I came, we waited a few minutes and fucked again. She didn't come either time. She said it was okay, that she never comes, but that she likes it anyway. Then she said she was thirsty, and I brought a glass of water from the kitchen for both of us. "This is your first time with a girl, eh?" she said, and stroked my face. I nodded. "That's really kinda cool," she said "That thank-you was totally . . . in another second, I would've thrown you out of here. But the fact that it's your first time is really kinda cool."

"My mom always says that 'thank you' are the only two words in the language that can never hurt," I said.

"So let your mom blow you," Vered said, and smiled, and I thought, "What a day. My first kiss. My first blow job. My first fuck. All on the same afternoon and all slightly miraculous. I was nineteen then, a soldier, which is late for a first kiss, maybe even for a first blow job. But I felt lucky. Because even if it took time, it had all finally happened, and with a nice girl who had the name of a flower.

Then Vered said she had a boyfriend. She said she didn't tell me before we kissed because a kiss is no big deal, even if there's a boyfriend, and she didn't tell me when she blew me because my prick was in her mouth. Anyway, when she finally did tell me, she also said that she hoped I wasn't offended or anything, because I look like I'm a little too sensitive. I told her that I was surprised, but not the least bit offended. Just the opposite, the fact that she had a boyfriend and still slept with me was even a little flattering. She laughed and said, "'Flattering' is a big word. I have a boyfriend, but he's a shit, and you . . . right from the first kiss I felt you were a virgin, and—what can you do—there's something cool about a virgin."

She told me that when she was a kid, her parents used to send her to camp during vacations, and at camp, after supper, the counselors used to toss giant bags of chips into the air and everyone tried to grab them in midair. "You have to understand," she said while stroking the five hairs that had grown on my chest, "there were enough chips for everyone, and we knew that, but there's nothing like that feeling of ripping open the bag and being the first one to eat from it."

"So now that I'm open," I said in a slightly choked voice, "I'm not worth anything anymore?"

"Don't exaggerate," Vered said, "but let's just say that you're worth a little less." I asked her when her parents were coming back, and she said not for another hour and a half at least. I asked her if she would agree to have sex with me again, and she slapped me. Not really hard, but enough to hurt, and said, "Don't say 'agree,' say 'want,' you asshole." And after a second of silence, she said, "You're like a camel, eh? You think that when you leave here there's a desert waiting for you outside, and who knows when you'll find water the next time." She took my prick in her hand and said, "Don't worry. It's not a desert.

Everyone fucks in this world and everyone'll keep fucking. Everyone. Even you."

After we fucked again, she walked me to the door, and after she opened it, she said, "If you meet me by accident at a falafel place or in the movies or at the mall with my boyfriend, don't pretend you don't know me, okay? I hate when people do that. Just say hello, the kind of normal hello you say to someone you know from the scouts, okay?" I asked her if we could see each other again, and she stroked my face and said I shouldn't be offended, but she couldn't because of Asi and everything. From that, I understood that her boyfriend's name was Asi.

I didn't plan to cry, but I did, and she said, "I've never met anyone as weird as you." I told her that I was crying with happiness, but she didn't believe me. "It's not a desert out there," she told me. "You'll see, you'll fuck your head off."

I never saw her again after that. Not in the movies. Not at a falafel place. Not at the mall. But if she ever happens to read this story, I'd like to thank her again.

TO: Sefi.Moreh
FROM: Michael.Warshavski
RE: RE: RE: RE: RE: RE: RE: RE: RE: RE: "Glitch at the Edge
  of the Galaxy" query

Dear Sefi,

I would like to thank you again for taking the trouble to open
your escape room this morning especially for my mother. In
general, the riddles were enjoyable, even if they were a bit
too easy (how many planets are there in our solar system—
really . . .) But the last one, the room which (if I understood
correctly) was supposed to resemble a flying saucer, was
frustrating and annoying. An escape room cannot presume
to be based on astronomical truths and, at the same time,
consider the existence of aliens to be a proven fact. It is
no wonder my mother could not solve the riddle, which
frustrated and saddened her very much. Furthermore, I
warmly recommend that you turn down the air-conditioning
in the room. It is supposed to be a journey to outer space, not
the North Pole.

With thanks,
Michael (Warshavski)

HOME

—•———————•—

It started when little Hillel was almost two years old. Yochai would try to drop him off and leave him at preschool, and little Hillel would yell, "Home! Home!" and hurl his body onto the cold floor, still yelling, "Home! Home!"

The teacher would tell Yochai to ignore it, to just leave, and Yochai, who from childhood had been one of those kids who did exactly what the teacher said, would take his bag and go.

The yelling started in preschool but continued at friends' houses and at his grandparents' homes, where there was no teacher around to supervise. Yochai caved in instantly, put little Hillel on his back, went out to the car, and drove home. Sometimes a grandmother would complain that they hadn't even eaten the leek patties she'd made or seen some cousin who was on his way and would be there in just another few minutes, but Yochai didn't even stay to listen. As he flew down the stairs, he'd say over his shoulder, "If we make him stay, it'll only get worse," and disappear. In his heart, he knew Hillel would calm down in a minute or two, the way he did in preschool, but there was something in those screams that fit perfectly with Yochai's wishes. And it wasn't that home was so great: their apartment was two and a half rooms in the older, northern part of the city, the kind of place that, in the newspaper for-rent ads, always included "renovation needed," at the bottom. Which didn't keep their landlord from demanding $1,800 a month, and getting it. Maybe because of the really good location. Central but quiet. Except for those nights when a woman who lived in the next building screamed.

The screaming neighbor's bedroom window was opposite theirs, and when she screamed, you couldn't sleep. "Rip me apart," she'd shriek. "Fuck my brains out!"

"What kind of person says things like that?" Hodaya would whisper angrily. "It sounds like a punk beating someone up, not like a woman making love." "Maybe she's not making love?" Yochai tried to defend her. "Maybe someone's just fucking her real hard?" The sounds she made didn't really sound like lovemaking, but more like wild shrieks of pain and pleasure that woke up everyone in both buildings. Even though none of the neighbors mentioned the screams to him, it was clear they were disruptive to everyone. It was as if those screams were a kind of pogrom that terrified the entire street, causing everyone to stay quietly in their apartments until the danger passed. Yochai really wanted to talk to someone about it but was embarrassed. Everyone seemed to be embarrassed. But there was a clear reason for Yochai's embarrassment. It was because he and Hodaya had nothing at all to scream about, so that whenever the woman screamed, it felt like a protest against their much less creative sex life. And it wasn't that he hadn't tried to learn things from her. He really did want to fuck his beloved Hodaya's brains out, but somehow everything with them was much tamer and more controlled. "Only animals have sex like that," Hodaya had once said about the neighbor, and a few days later, when Yochai and Hodaya were fucking, Yochai tried to imagine he was a bear or a tiger or a dog, but apart from the fact that he bit the back of Hodaya's neck, which made her very angry, nothing changed.

Hillel also woke up when the neighbor screamed. Yochai knew because he saw him standing in his crib, listening. But the screaming never made Hillel cry; he just stood and listened, fascinated. When the fucking was over, he would lie down again, murmur unclear things to himself, and fall back to sleep.

It happened on a rainy winter day, when they came back from preschool. When Yochai opened the door, Hillel ran past him into the living room and looked around: he looked at the toy chest filled with half-broken plastic and electronic toys. He looked at the awful paintings they'd had to hang on the living room walls because they were painted by Hodaya's late brother. He looked at the tired, threadbare kitchen floor mat that looked like the lone survivor of a terrible floor mat holocaust. Hillel threw his tiny body onto the cold floor tiles and yelled, "Home! Home!" At first, Yochai tried to argue. To explain that they were already home and everything was okay. But it didn't work. Not only because Hillel didn't listen but also because, in his heart, Yochai himself wasn't really convinced. That sad apartment wasn't really a home, and to say that everything was okay was an exaggeration. Yochai very quickly found himself picking up the boy, taking him to the car, buckling him into his booster seat, and starting to drive. "Home! Home!" Hillel kept screaming, and Yochai, trying to smile at him through the rearview mirror, said, "Daddy's looking for it." They drove up the coast to Herzliya but didn't find anything on the way that was even close to a home, and they didn't turn back until Hillel tired himself out from screaming and fell asleep.

When they returned, a small miracle happened and Yochai found parking right in front of the building. Just as he took Hillel gently out of his booster seat and put him on his shoulder, he noticed that the woman from the next building and the guy who fucked her brains out were standing on the sidewalk, looking at him. They were both carrying full plastic bags from the supermarket. "What a sweetie," the woman whispered, putting her bags down on the sidewalk. She bent forward to caress Hillel but stopped before touching him. "It's okay," Yochai said with a smile, "you can touch him, he won't wake up. He's a sound sleeper." The woman stroked Hillel's curly hair, and the boy trembled slightly in his sleep. That was the first time Yochai saw her close up and not just as a moving shadow on the balcony. She was thin and had terrible skin, and her face seemed set in a smile. "Is he your youngest?" the guy who fucked her brains out asked. He was almost completely bald and looked twenty years older than her. "He's our only one," Yochai apologized, "for the time being." The guy who fucked her brains out said he had four with someone who didn't talk to him anymore, and the oldest one was in the army already. "There's nothing better than kids," he said, running his hand over the little hair he had left.

The neighbor and the father of four went off, leaving Yochai standing with Hillel in his arms, looking at the lighted window of their living room from the outside. He knew that Hodaya had already come home from school and must be very worried. Only now did he realize that when he carried the screaming Hillel to the car with him, he forgot to take his cell phone. She must have tried to call him. When he went inside, she'd be angry, but she'd forgive him soon enough and cry and tell him how frightened she'd been that something happened. It really was wrong of him to take Hillel like that without letting her know. If it had been the other way around, he would have been scared, too. Hillel had slipped down a little in his arms, and Yochai pushed him up higher on his shoulder and walked toward the building entrance. The air smelled nice after the rain, and Hillel, pressed up against his body, felt just like a hot water bottle. Yochai allowed himself a long moment on the dark street, then took a last deep breath before he continued into the lobby.

TO: Chief.Department.of.Rational.Species.Study
FROM: Field.Agent.SEFI
RE: Escape Room—Destroying evidence of extraterrestrial
  presence

After five months of genetic surveillance and examination of visitors to the escape room under my management, it has been decided to cut off all contact with the species under discussion. The last encounter with the earthling known as "Warshavski" tipped the scales absolutely. The same aggressiveness and arrogance we saw during previous observations were evident in the aforementioned native with menacing force, and as I point out in the attached report, if those patterns of behavior are commonplace in the rest of the species, an open relationship with them might result in the end of our species. All evidence of extraterrestrial presence at coordinates 66:22:14 (local name "Rishon Lezion Meadows Shopping Mall") has been destroyed, and I am starting my journey back to the mother planet.

Molecularly yours,
Field Agent SEFI, solar system

PINEAPPLE CRUSH

———•————•———

The first hit is the one that colors your world. Save it for the evening—and any piece of trash flickering across your TV screen will be riveting. Puff it at midday, before you get on your bike, and the world around you will feel like one big adventure. Smoke it as soon as you wake up in the morning, before your coffee, and it'll give you the energy to crawl out of bed or dive back in for another few hours of sleep.

The first hit of the day is like a childhood friend, a first love, a commercial for life. But it's different from life itself, which is something that, if I could have, I would have returned to the store ages ago. In the commercial it's made-to-order, all-inclusive, finger-licking, carefree living. After that first one, more hits will come along to help you soften reality and make the day tolerable, but they won't feel the same.

I always take my first hit at sundown. The after-school program where I work is half a mile from the beach, and I finish at five, when Raviv's sweaty mother, who always gets there last, finally comes to pick up her snot-nosed second-grader. That leaves me time to run errands, if I have any, then to grab a coffee on Ben Yehuda or HaYarkon, and mosey over to the promenade. That's where I eagerly wait for the sun to kiss the sea, the way a kid waits for his good-night kiss, the way a pimply teenager slow-dancing at prom waits for his first French kiss, the way a wrinkly old man waits for a wet peck on the cheek from his grandchild. The second the sun starts reflecting off the water, I pull out the joint from my pack of Noblesse cigarettes and light up.

I smoke that joint quietly. I try to be in the moment, to feel the breeze on my face, to take pleasure in the colors of the sky and the way the sea sizzles in the red sunlight. I try, but I can't really do it, because as soon as I take the first puff, my mind starts letting in all kinds of thoughts about how it was a mistake to call that first-grader Romi "poop face," because the little snitch will tell her bitch of a mother about it, and she'll go straight to the principal. And about how the tall, skinny second-grade teacher is nicer to me than the other teachers are, always smiling and asking how I am, so maybe something could happen there. And also about my rich asshole brother who keeps working over Mom to make her stop helping me out with my rent, like it's any of his business. I always try to lose those thoughts and not waste the best hit of the day on them, and sometimes I can do it. But even when I can't, I figure if you're going to think bad thoughts about your brother, you may as well be high while you're doing it.

Life is like an ugly low table left in your living room by the previous tenants. Most of the time you notice it and you're careful, you remember it's there, but sometimes you forget and then you get the pointy corner right in your shin or your kneecap, and it hurts. And it almost always leaves a scar. When you smoke, it doesn't make that low table disappear. Nothing except death can make it disappear. But a good puff can file down the corners, round them off a little. And then when you get whacked, it hurts a lot less.

After I finish smoking, I get on my bike and take a little spin around town. I watch people. And if I see someone really interesting—and that someone is almost always a she—I follow her and make up a little story: The person who just got yelled at over the phone by the tanned woman I'm following is her younger sister who's always making eyes at her husband at Friday-night dinners; the pint of ice cream she picked up at the corner store is for her spoiled brat of a son; and the drugstore stop is for the Pill, so she doesn't accidentally have another spoiled brat. After that, if the weather's decent, I plunk myself on a bench on Ben Gurion Boulevard and smoke a regular cigarette, and I sit there as long as the high or some bit of it is still going. When it completely fades, I jump on my bike and head back to my apartment to the TV, to Tinder, computer games, trance music.

For four years, I've been taking my first drag at sundown. Barely missed an evening. There were a few anomalous puffs that managed to convince me to light up earlier in the day, but nothing major. And that is something that a suggestible, addictive personality like me can certainly be proud of. More than one thousand puffs on Frishman Beach at sunset. More than one thousand uninterrupted puffs until she came along. With her "Excuse me?" so soft and gentle that even before I turned around I knew she would be ugly, because pretty girls don't have to try so hard to be gentle: people do whatever they want anyway.

She was older than me, about forty. White blouse, black skirt. Brown hair tied back. Smart eyes. Glistening complexion, a few wrinkles, mainly under the eyes, but they only made her sexier.

I wanted to ask if I could help, but because I was smoking, the only sound that came out was a slightly aggressive "What?" I think it sounded aggressive, because she took a step back and said, "I'm sorry, nothing." I cleared my throat and said, "No, it's okay, tell me. What did you want to ask?" She smiled shyly and half whispered: "I wanted to ask if that's pot." She didn't look like someone who stopped people on the street to ask them a thing like that, and she definitely didn't look like a cop. So I nodded. "Can I have some?" she asked, and held out two fingers. Her hand was shaking.

I handed it to her. She tried to inhale and say thanks at the same time. It ended with a splutter. We both grinned. Giving

up on the thanks, she took a long drag and held it in, like someone diving underwater. I hadn't seen anyone smoke that way
for years, like a kid smoking a cigarette. She tried to give the
joint back but I signaled for her to keep smoking. After another
few puffs she tried to give it back again, and this time I took it.
We smoked together. When the joint was done, the sun had
already set. "Wow," she said, "I haven't smoked for so many
years that I forgot how much fun it is." I wanted to say something clever, but the only response I could come up with was
that it was good stuff. She nodded and said thanks. I said she
was welcome and she walked away.

That was it. It was supposed to end there. But like I already
said, when I'm high I follow people, especially women, and so
I followed her. She walked to Ben Yehuda, where she bought a
bottle of mango-flavored "Island" juice. From Ben Yehuda she
took a cab. I followed the cab and saw her get out at the Akirov
Towers, walk into the lobby of one of them, and say hello to the
doorman. Forty years old, pressed white blouse, Akirov—not
exactly the kind of woman you'd expect to share a spliff with on
the beach.

On the way home I told myself I should have hit on her.
Asked for her phone number. My greedy brain kept scolding
me for not trying to take advantage of the situation, to get
something out of it, but then my heart said very clearly that it
would have been not cool to do that. She asked me for a drag,
that's what she wanted, and, yes, I could have tried to get somewhere with her, but the fact that sometimes when a woman

smiles at me on the street I can just smile back without trying to cash in on it actually says something good about me. Maybe about her, too, considering that's what she brought out in me.

The day after I get high with Akirov, I finish work early. Raviv's mom comes to pick him up at four fifteen because they have a doctor's appointment with a specialist. In the thirty seconds it takes her to put a sweatshirt and backpack on her booger-smeared kid, she manages to say the word "specialist" five times. Except that not one of those five times does she say what he's a specialist in. Maybe snot.

I hop on my bike and get to the beach earlier than usual. I grab a bench and sit there people watching to pass the time until sunset. There's not much foot traffic. Tourists in T-shirts and sweatpants, gushing about how nice it is in February in Tel Aviv. Israelis on their cell phones, hurrying somewhere without even noticing that they're by the sea. When the first ray of sun scratches the waves, I don't light up yet. And even though I'm super-horny for that first puff, I wait another three or four minutes before I start. I don't even know why.

While I smoke, I do what I always do: I look at the sea, try to live in the moment, let the beauty sink in. But thoughts fly around my head in all directions. I imagine Raviv at the specialist's. Maybe he has something terminal. Poor kid. All the kids at after-school torment him. I do, too. I call him Snotface, and I've mimicked him wiping his nose on his sleeve. I promise myself I'm going to stop, and the thoughts go back to her again. Akirov. Some part of me was hoping she'd come again today, but it's weird enough when someone you don't know asks to smoke with you, just like that, right on the promenade—what are the chances of it happening two days in a row? I finish smoking and keep sitting there until the sun completely sinks into the sea. It's not nice of me to call her Akirov. So what if she lives in a luxury building? That's just stereotyping. Like calling an Arab "Arab," or a Russian "Russian." Although, when I think about it, that's exactly what I always do. I'm getting cold now. It was hot in the afternoon so I didn't bring a jacket.

I've already stood up and taken a step toward my bike when I see her coming. She hasn't seen me yet. I turn my back to her and start digging through my pockets. I usually roll only one joint ahead of time, but today I have two, because I promised to bring one for Yuri, the Russian security guard who stands at the school gates. He never turned up for his shift, so I still have it in my pack. I pull out the second joint and light it, all casual, like I'm not already high as a kite from the first one. I take two quick drags, still with my back to her, and then I turn around. She's really close now, maybe twenty steps away, but she hasn't spotted me yet. She's on the phone. It's a grim conversation, I can tell. I've had enough of them in my life to recognize one. She hangs up right as she walks past me. It looks like she's crying. I follow her. Fast. But I don't run. I don't want to look too eager. When I'm right next to her I say, "Excuse me?" but in an American accent. Like those old American Jews who always say "Shalom?" and when you stop to see what's up, they speak to you in English. She looks at me. No recognition. "You dropped this," I say, and hold out the joint. Now the lightbulb goes on. She smiles and takes it. When she's right in front of me like that and I can see her eyes, I can tell for sure she's been crying. "Wow," she says, "you came just when I needed you. Like an angel." "What do you mean, like?" I say, "I am an angel. God put me on the promenade today just for you." She smiles again and blows out a little cloud of smoke: "The angel of weed?" "I'm the angel who makes wishes come true," I tell her. "Five minutes ago a little girl wanted a Popsicle, and before that it was a blind guy who wanted to see. I can't help it that I landed a pothead." I manage to make her laugh. Or rather, the combination of the pot and me manages to make her laugh. She's happy, Akirov. And I feel happy with her, briefly useful to humanity.

When the joint is finished, she says thanks and asks which direction I'm going in, and I realize that while we were smoking I kept walking with her and got far away from my bike. I consider lying, but then I decide to confess. I tell her my bike is tied up back where we met.

"Do you come here every day?" she asks.

I nod. "And you?"

"I have to." She shrugs and points south to the corncob skyscraper. "I work there."

I tell her I always come to the promenade after work, to light up a joint with the sunset. A girl once told me that watching the sunset opens up your heart, and my heart's been closed for a long time, so I come here every day to try to open it up.

"But today you were late," Akirov says, glancing at the time on her phone.

"Today I was late," I concur, "which is a good thing. Otherwise we wouldn't have met."

"So if I come here tomorrow at sunset, will you share with me again?"

I pause for a second and scrutinize her. Maybe something's there, maybe she's hitting on me. But I can see she isn't. It's just the pot. Even today, when I stopped her, she only recognized me by the pot. "Sure. It's more fun to smoke with someone nice than alone anyway."

For five days me and Akirov have been smoking at sunset. Five days, and I still know almost nothing about her, not even her name. I know she's vegetarian but sometimes eats sushi, and that she speaks good English, and French, too, because this pain-in-the-ass French tourist came up to us the day before yesterday and Akirov explained to her in fluent French how to get to the port. I also know she's married, even though she doesn't wear a ring, because on one of our first days she told me that her husband doesn't let her smoke pot because it's illegal and because it screws up your short-term memory. "And what do you say to that?" I asked. I wanted to see if I could get her to spill any dirt on her husband. "I don't have a problem with it being illegal," she said, shrugging. "And the short-term memory thing? To be honest, it's not like I have such great short-term memories to preserve anyway." Well, that was almost a complaint. Either way, it was obvious there was something weighing on her. Something she didn't talk about even when she was stoned, which for me was the sign of a strong person. Strong and not a whiner. That—and the thing that happened with the fascist vice cop yesterday.

It was the first time a cop had ever come up to me while I was smoking, and this guy was an especially creepy one. Short but muscular, with a neck as thick as a utility pole and a tight plaid shirt with cut-off sleeves. He shoved his badge in my face and wondered in a cocky voice if he could ask what I was smoking. Akirov, without missing a beat, pulled the joint out of my mouth, took a drag, blew smoke right into his face, and said, "Marlboro Lights." She tossed the joint over the railing onto the sand below, and just as swiftly pulled out a pack of Marlboro Lights from her pocket, lit one, and held out the pack: "Want one?"

The cop flicked her hand away. "What do you think?" he screamed. "You think I'm retarded?"

"I'd rather not answer that," she said with a sweet smile, "because I am a law-abiding citizen, and insulting an officer of the public is a crime."

"ID! Show me your ID right now!"

Akirov pulled out her driver's license and also handed the cop a business card. "Keep this," she said, "I'm a lawyer. And judging by your face, it's only a matter of time before you beat the crap out of a Palestinian and need legal counsel."

"I know your firm," the cop said as he dropped her card on the path. "You guys'll defend any shithead if he has enough money."

"True," said Akirov, jerking her head at the tossed card, "but once in a while we also defend shitheads pro bono."

The cop didn't answer. He went over to the railing and peered down at the sand strewn with trash. You could see from the look on his face that he was debating whether or not to jump down and try to find our roach among the dozens that littered the beach. "Don't give up," Akirov called out, "if you look carefully you'll find it in an hour at most. And if you take it to forensics they may even be able to isolate my fingerprints, and then you can go to your commissioner and tell him you want to press charges for a marijuana roach. Which is maybe not quite the same as solving a double homicide, but hey . . ." "Bitch," the cop muttered without thinking, and Akirov continued, "An officer of the law cursing at a lawyer, on the other hand, is a slightly more serious offense." She winked at me when she said that. "Okay, get the hell outta here," the cop snapped. I started moving toward my bike but Akirov grabbed my hand and held me back. "You get the hell out, Popeye," she told him, "before I decide to ask for your details and report you to Internal Affairs." The cop gave us a violent glare, and my instincts told me to make myself scarce, but Akirov's hand around mine told me to stay put. Her clammy palm made me realize she was stressed.

That was the only sign. The cop hissed something and walked off, and when he was far enough away, she leaned over and picked up the card. "Dumbass," she murmured, "we lost half a joint because of him." With an expert hand she tore off a strip of the card to use as a filter. "You have enough on you for another one?" she asked. I almost said that I didn't but that I lived nearby and we could go over to my place, but something about her wouldn't let me lie. So we rolled another one, sitting on a promenade bench. A third of her business card became a filter. The other two thirds, which said "Iris Kaisman, Attorney," stayed in my pocket.

On Friday evening I'm at my mom's for dinner. My older brother, Hagai, comes, too, with his daughter, Naomi. You can tell from the second they walk in that they're half fighting. It's not hard to fight with my brother. He's one of those people who are always sure they know everything. He's been that way since we were born, and the boatloads of money he made in the tech industry have only made things worse. Not even the wallop he got two years ago when Sandy, Naomi's mother, died of cancer, did anything to soften it. Naomi's seventeen now, a beautiful, tall girl, like her late mother, and even though she has braces, she doesn't look or sound like a child for even a second. At dinner she tells us excitedly about a species of dwarf jellyfish that lives forever. This jellyfish matures, mates, then becomes a baby again, and it goes on like that ad infinitum. "It'll never die!" Naomi gushes, and the mixture of enthusiasm and braces makes her spit on Hagai and me a little bit. "Think about it—if we can study its genetic composition thoroughly, then maybe we'll be able to live forever, too."

I grin at her. "To tell you the truth, even sixty or seventy years sounds like too long to me."

My brother explains that Naomi wants to go to Stanford next year and get her degree in biology.

"Wonderful!" my mom exclaims. "You'll be brilliant."

"What do you mean, 'wonderful'? I told her she can do her army service first, like everyone else, and when she's done I'll pay for her to study whatever she wants."

"Not an option. The army has nothing to offer me," Naomi says.

"It has nothing to offer you? It's the army, it's not a branch of Zara! No one goes there because of the selection or the styles. You think income tax has anything to offer me? No, but I still pay it every month. Isn't that so?" Hagai glances at me, expecting me to intervene on his behalf. Not because he's always been such a great brother and I owe him. He hasn't. But because he's so right.

"Nothing bad will happen if you skip the army," I tell Naomi. "The world will be better off with you studying jellyfish than spending two years making coffee for some horny officer."

"Yeah, take your uncle's advice," Hagai hisses, "he's really gone far in life."

After dinner, when Hagai and Naomi are gone, my mom gives me another slice of cake and asks if everything's okay and if I'm seeing anyone. I tell her everything's fine, that they're pretty pleased with me at school, and I'm dating a lawyer. I almost never lie to my mom. She's the only one who has to accept me as I am, so there's no need, but this lie isn't for her. It's for me. It's for those few minutes when I get to imagine I have a life different from the one I really have. When I warm up at night in bed with someone who isn't "divorced, looking for a non-committed relationship" whom I dug up on a dating app. At the door my mom says, "You know Hagai didn't mean it," and when she hugs me she puts some bills in my jeans pocket. Whenever Hagai lays into me, she gives me a few hundred shekels. It's starting to feel like my side job.

I take a cab to the bodega next to my apartment and buy a cheap bottle of whiskey, which the Ethiopian checkout guy with the dyed-blond hair swears came from Scotland even though the label is in Russian. At home I finish off half the bottle. Then a slender forty-six-year-old from Tinder comes over. Before we fuck she tells me it's important to her that she be honest and inform me that she has cancer and it might be terminal. Then she takes a deep breath and says, "That's it. I've said it. If you're not comfortable, we don't have to do it." "I'm totally comfortable," I say, and when she comes she screams so loud that the upstairs neighbor bangs on my door. Afterward we smoke a cigarette together, a regular one, and she takes a cab home.

———————

Sundays are usually my least favorite day of the week. It wasn't always this way, only since I started working. Before the after-school program I did nothing for five years, and then I hated all days equally. Honestly, most of the time I couldn't really tell the difference. When I got up at midday, I would look at my watch and wonder if I had any hash or weed or money left and if I remembered where I'd put my cell phone and keys. Questions like "What day is today?" hardly ever came up, and other than Fridays, when I went to see my mom, the whole rest of the week felt like one big, sticky glob of sleep-wake-eat-shit-TV and the occasional fuck.

My job set things straight. It separated the days out. Mondays started to mean darbouka class and the pretty counselor with the tongue piercing, and Wednesdays meant meatballs in sweet tomato sauce in the cafeteria, which the kids hated but always reminded me of Grandma Geula's cooking. And Thursdays were soccer in the yard and the kids looking at me like I was Cristiano Ronaldo and not just a tired grown-up who could barely outsmart a bunch of seven-year-olds. And then shitty Sundays with the quasi-Nazi roll call put on by Maor, the guy who runs the after-school program, who always had a bad word for each of the counselors before he disappeared from our lives for another week. After my chill Saturdays, that always rubbed me the wrong way.

But this week, for the first time since I started work, I was looking forward to Sunday. To the sunset, to the promenade, to getting high with Akirov. And it wasn't out of horniness or anxiety about how maybe I'd say something and she'd come over to my place. It was that I genuinely missed her. I missed someone I didn't even really know. And that was exciting and at the same time humiliating. Because that feeling of missing someone was mostly evidence of how vapid my life had become.

Except Akirov didn't come on Sunday. I waited for her till it got dark—long after, in fact. She didn't come on Monday or Tuesday, either. While I smoked alone, I reminded myself that she was just a random woman who'd shared a joint with me on the promenade a few times, not my fiancée or someone I'd donated a kidney to or anything. But it didn't do any good.

On Wednesday, after the kids finish wrangling their lukewarm meatballs, I realize Raviv isn't there. I never count them, even though Maor says we're supposed to count them every hour. But when someone's missing, I usually figure it out, so I ask Yuri, who says he saw a few kids go behind the gym. They're not allowed to leave the classroom without permission, and by the time I get to the gym I've had time to think up the punishment I'll give Raviv, feel sorry for him, and cancel it. Behind the gym, in the long-jump sand pit, I see Raviv crying, and not far away from him I see Liam, the meanest kid in my group, lying facedown in the sand while some fat redhead whose face

I've seen before sits on top of him and punches him in the back. He's punching the way a kid does: lots of anger, very little technique. Without even knowing how things got to this point, I'm with the redhead. I've felt like punching Liam myself a bunch of times. The kid doesn't talk, he just gives orders, and even that he does in a shitty way. Every other line out of his mouth is about how he's going to tell Mom, or the teacher, or the principal.

The redhead keeps pounding on Liam, and I know I should run over and separate them. The fact that they disappeared from the classroom is my screwup, and now I'm really going to get in trouble, especially with Liam's mom being on the parent council. But as I watch the redhead railing on him, a little voice inside me tells me to wait a while longer, just till he lands one really good punch.

This has not been a good week. Not good at all. All that embarrassing waiting around for Akirov. I didn't even try to bring a single girl home. This fight is without a doubt the highlight of my tedious week, and another few seconds of enjoyment aren't going to hurt anyone. While I think all this, the redhead gets off Liam's back, and just when I think the whole thing has played itself out, he takes a step back and slams his foot on Liam's head. As I start running, I realize Raviv is on to me. He saw me watching the fight that whole time without doing anything. I sprint the few feet between me and the redhead as fast as I can, both because I'm stressed and to confuse Raviv a little, so he'll think afterward that he must have been wrong: it wasn't possible that I was standing there watching instead of breaking them up and that I took off so fast.

When I get to the redhead I shove him hard enough to move him off Liam and I yell, "What are you doing? Are you out of your mind?" Then I bend over to check on Liam, and all that time out of the corner of my eye I can see Raviv watching me. Liam's upper lip is bleeding and he looks unconscious. The redhead stands there wailing. He says Liam cheated him on Trashies and when he asked him to give back his cards, Liam told him he had poop-colored eyes and his dad was unemployed. From the way the redhead says it, I can tell he doesn't even know what "unemployed" means. I try to talk to Liam and shake him gently, but he doesn't respond, and I get really nervous. I tell the panicky redhead not to move and I run to the water fountain. On my way back I can hear Liam up and screaming, "You're finished at this school, you fat-face loser! My mom'll make sure of that!" Liam is sitting on the ground with his hands on his face, and the redhead stands next to him, shaking all over, really sobbing now. Suddenly Yuri turns up. I'd left the kids alone in the classroom and one of them found a lighter in my bag and set fire to a poster of Yitzhak Rabin in the hallway. Yuri's account of how he put out the smoldering poster makes it sounds like, at the very least, he'd saved a baby from a burning house. I splash water on Liam's face. He looks all right now and his lip is hardly bleeding anymore. The redhead keeps blubbering, but I'm not interested in him. What I am interested in is that snot-faced

Raviv, who doesn't take his eyes off me even after we go back into the classroom. I call Liam's dad, who works as a land surveyor and is usually at home, and he gets there in five minutes. Liam screams that he took too long and he's going to tell on him to Mom, and then he tells him about the redhead. He embellishes a lot, and says the redhead hit him on the head with a rock, but I don't intervene. As long as he doesn't start in on me, I figure I'm better off keeping quiet. Then the mom of the twins with the unibrows arrives. She has a South American accent. She had the twins through IVF and, judging by the way they turned out, she must have used a caveman's sperm.

Eventually it's just me and Raviv. I let him play on my iPhone, even though I never do that, and while he annihilates entire species on a game I downloaded a few days ago, I try to talk to him about what happened. "It's not okay that you and Liam ran away from class without permission," I tell him, but I say it pretty gently, like a kind mother, so he'll know I'm not against him but at the same time he'll understand I have something on him. "I won't tell your mom," I continue, "but I want you to promise not to do that again."

And this kid, without even looking up from the phone, says, "I saw you."

"Saw me what?" I ask, like I have no clue what he's talking about.

"I saw you while Gavri was beating up Liam. You were smiling."

"No I wasn't. I wasn't smiling. I ran. I ran as fast as I could to break it up."

But Raviv isn't with me anymore, he's in the game. Shooting lasers at anything that moves.

When his mom gets there, I don't call her out for being late like I usually do. I just tell her, "You have a really good kid. He's a sweetheart." Right next to him, so he can hear.

In the five minutes it takes me to get to the promenade, I have two unanswered calls and a text message from Maor. The message is blank. The fucker was too lazy to write anything, but he wanted me to see it and call him back. I debate whether to have a smoke first and then call him, or the other way around. The pro of smoking first is that the reefer will soften the discussion, envelop the whole unpleasantness in styrofoam and bubble wrap. The con is that I'll need to be sharp with him. I'll have to answer fast, maybe make up a lie or two right on the spot. I go with the second option and call him cold sober.

Maor yells at me: Liam's mother called and vowed to get all the other parents on board and make sure he loses the program next year. She's been compiling a list of complaints on him all year and she's going to make everything public, including the fact that the lunches are sometimes served frozen. Maor says that if she pulls it off, this whole episode could cost him two hundred thousand shekels and it's all my fault. Her kid won't be at school tomorrow because he has a concussion, and Maor wants me to go visit him before work and take him some candy or a toy, and suck up to his mom so she'll get off his case. The whole phone call is a total drag. He repeats everything ten times. I wish I'd smoked first. Before he hangs up he threatens me again. He says if they take away his license, he'll sue me. I tell him to calm down and I promise to go over tomorrow and kiss the mom's ass. By the time the call is done I've missed the sunset. I sit there in the dark, staring out at the sea, fully sober. Once the sun has set, there's nothing in that spot apart from ugly tourists and lousy music from the restaurants on the beach. And the next day I have to set my alarm clock and get up early so I'll have time to buy a gift for my least-favorite kid in the world. This week started off lousy and it's only gone downhill.

"I thought you left after sunset." I hear her voice and I feel—or at least imagine—her breath on the back of my neck.

"Sunrise, sunset—I've been waiting for you since Sunday," I reply with a smile, and then I get mad at myself because instead of saying something positive I managed to sound like a whiner and a doormat all at once.

"Sorry." Akirov sits down next to me. "Work was a shit show this week. Not just work—life, too."

I want to ask her what happened but I can sense she doesn't want to talk about it. So instead of drilling on about it, I take out a joint. After one puff I pass it to her and she sucks it up like a junkie. "I've been thinking about this drag for five days," she says, smiling, and hands it back to me. I don't take it. "You smoke it," I tell her, "smoke it to death." She hesitates for a second and then takes another toke. "Tough week?" I ask. She nods and sniffles. I'm not sure if she has a cold or if she's trying not to cry. "My week wasn't so hot, either," I say. "It's bad for us to not see each other for so long. It throws a wrench in our karma."

She smiles. "Listen, I want to ask you for a favor . . ." She digs through her bag while she talks, and I try to guess what she could possibly want from me. "I want to hire you." She takes out her wallet.

"As what?" I give her a big grin. "Your bodyguard? Babysitter for your kid? Personal chef?"

"I don't have a kid," she says with a sigh, "I'm not into food, and I'm pretty good at taking care of myself. I want to hire you to keep doing exactly what you do: come here every day at sunset, and wait for me if I'm late. Not long. An hour at most. And then smoke with me." While she talks, she counts out the money. "Here." She hands me a stack of hundreds. "There's two thousand here. Two thousand for three weeks. What do you say?"

"What do I say?" I repeat her question to buy time. "I say that I come here every sunset anyway, and smoking with you is more fun than smoking alone, so it's great that you want to pay me for spending a pleasant fifteen minutes with you on the beach when you have time, but taking money for talking to a friend . . ."

"But that's just it—we're not friends. And three weeks from

now I'm going to vanish from this place and you'll never see me again. These three weeks are going to be the toughest ones of my life. The daily joint with you will help make them a little bit easier." Her hand with the money is still held out. When she says we're not friends, it hurts. It hurts because it's true. I try to ignore it and focus only on the pragmatic stuff.

"If you want, I can buy you some weed for a couple of hundred shekels. At the rate you smoke, it'll last you more than three weeks."

"But I don't want you to buy it for me. I want you to smoke it with me. I can't keep weed around. I promised my husband I'd stop buying it."

"You promised him you wouldn't smoke," I correct her.

"I know," she says, and suddenly she starts crying, "But it's different with you. Even if he finds out, it'll be like I just met you on the street and you happened to be smoking so I had a drag, too. It's not the same as buying . . ."

I take the money. I don't want her to cry. "Okay, boss, we have a deal." I give her a wink. "But the two grand only covers drugs. Sex and rock 'n' roll are extra."

She laughs, and the laughter and tears come out together. I don't know what she's going through, but it sounds like some serious drama, and even though there's nothing going on between us, I really want to help her. "I only have one condition," I add as I shove the money into my wallet, "I want you to tell me why you're disappearing in three weeks. When you said that, the way you said it, it didn't sound like a good kind of disappearance. And, speaking as . . . your employee, I have a right to know."

"I'll tell you," she says, and wipes her face with her hand. "I promise. But not today."

The alarm clock on my phone wakes me at eleven. I brush my teeth, shave, and roll a joint for the evening. I do everything fast. I still have to pick up something for Liam and go by his house, and I only have an hour and a half. It's a good thing he lives near the school.

His mother opens the door wearing a pink tracksuit and a sour face. "I came to check on Liam," I say, trying to sound like I care.

"It's a pity you didn't check on him yesterday, before he was brutally beaten," she retorts in her low, sludgy voice. "I still don't understand how a child can disappear from the classroom for almost an hour without anyone noticing."

My instinct is to say something about how it's easier to look after kids who respect other people than ones who keep lying and running away, but I remember my talk with Maor, so instead I explain apologetically that yesterday a child brought a lighter to school and tried to burn some posters in the hallway, and since I was busy taking care of this unusual incident, it took me a while to realize that Liam was gone. "I just want you to know, Mrs. Rosner, that I didn't sleep all night because of what happened. It was a terrible mistake and I want to apologize to you."

"I'm not the one you should apologize to," she says in a voice that sounds slightly less furious. "I'm not the one who was beaten unconscious and is still suffering from aches all over my body. You should apologize to Liam." She takes me to the little shit, who's sitting up in his parents' bed, watching a Japanese anime series—a soccer match between robots and aliens. Other than a slightly puffy lip, he looks totally fine. "Liam," his mother says in a teacherly tone, "you have a visitor."

"Not now," Liam says without taking his eyes off the screen, "I'm in the middle."

"He brought you a present," she says, trying to tempt him. "Lego Space!"

"I hate Lego."

"Hey, Liam," I jump in, "I came to see how you're feeling."

"I'm in the middle," he says, still not moving his eyes off the screen. "Did you get a gift receipt for the Lego?"

At the door, Liam's mother thanks me for visiting and says she has a meeting with the principal and Maor tomorrow and that she's not planning to let this slide. "Liam has three older brothers," she says in a pathos-filled tone, "and as a parent, I have never come across such an extreme incident: a seven-year-old boy attacked with rocks and sticks without anyone intervening."

I realize the last thing I should do is get into an argument with her, so I just nod. I tell her that if I were a parent I would react exactly the same way. "You have a lovely boy, Mrs. Rosner, and, thank God, he came through this whole thing without serious harm. That's what really matters." Walking down the steps, I text Maor to say I made the visit and the mom is still pissed, but I'm confident she'll calm down before the meeting. He doesn't answer, which is a good sign. When Maor texts or calls, it's always bad.

The afternoon at work goes by without incident, but it's tense. All the parents who come to pick up their kids throw out something: they're worried, this is not okay. They're not blaming me personally, but they're unhappy with the program and the school. The twins' mother says that in Buenos Aires they'd have at least two counselors for this number of children. Noya's father, who is an officer in the navy and always wears his uniform when he comes to pick her up, says it all starts with education at home. I murmur agreement with everything they say, and try to look contrite. There's obviously going to be loads of yelling and threats at the meeting tomorrow, but if I know this school, nothing serious will come of it. They'll suspend the redhead for a few days, they may even expel him if his parents are weak or suckers, but it looks like I'll survive—as long as Raviv doesn't talk.

Raviv and I are the last ones there, as usual. I tell him I downloaded an upgrade for the game he likes and ask if he wants to play. He smiles and holds out his hand for my phone. Before I give it to him, I explain that it's fine with me for him to play, but it has to be a secret, because if he tells the other kids they'll want to play, too, and I can't let everyone do it. Raviv thinks for a moment and then nods. I give him the iPhone and he starts the game. While he plays, I ask him if he's good at keeping secrets. He doesn't answer. I don't know if it's because of the question or because he's absorbed in the game. After a few seconds the iPhone makes a happy tune—he must have leveled up.

"Way to go! You're really good at this!" I exclaim.

"Why did you smile while Liam was getting beaten up?" He doesn't even look up from the screen when he asks me that.

Now it's my turn to keep quiet. My instinct tells me to make something up. My instinct always tells me to make something up. But just like with Akirov, I ignore it. "I did it because I don't like him," I finally say. "Lots of times he's done bad things that I thought he should be punished for and he always gets away with it, and when I saw Gavri hitting him—I know this isn't a nice thing to say, but I was glad."

Raviv looks up and stares at me. The game keeps running and I hear him getting eliminated, but he doesn't seem to care. "What did he do? What things did he do that you thought he should be punished for?"

"Lots of things. But mostly it bothers me that he picks on the weak kids."

Raviv wipes his nose with the back of his hand without taking his eyes off me. "But he's not the only one who picks on weak kids." He doesn't say it, but we both know he means me.

"That's true, and it's a horrible thing to do."

"Then why do you do it?" He doesn't look angry at all, just curious.

I shrug my shoulders. "I don't know. Maybe because most of the time I feel weak myself, and when I pick on someone, I feel stronger."

Raviv nods. He seems to understand me.

It's cold on the promenade that evening, and there's a gusty wind. The sky is completely black and it looks like it's about to storm. I huddle in my coat and wait for Akirov. It's my first day as her employee. She's late, but not by very much. She's wearing a wool hat. I don't usually like girls with hats—it always makes them look like a character on a kids' show. But on her the hat sits really well. It brings out the green in her eyes.

It's too windy to light up, so I suggest we find a lobby somewhere. While we smoke together in the doorway of a decrepit building on HaYarkon Street, it starts raining, and I think about my bike getting wet on the promenade. "What a crappy day," I say, and she nods, as though something that belongs to her is also getting wet out there. I tell her about my day, and the whole story with Liam and his mother. She asks if I like my job. I think for a moment—no one's ever asked me that. "I don't know if I'd use the word 'like,'" I finally answer, "but I definitely prefer it to working with adults. With kids, you can take a bite out of their sandwich or you can tickle them. With adults it's more complicated."

She takes a sandwich wrapped in paper out of her bag. "Want some? I made it this morning. It's tuna fish."

I tell her I'm not hungry and ask if I can tickle her instead.

She smiles. "Do you think you'll get fired?" She takes a bite out of her sandwich.

"I don't know. I'll find out after the meeting with Maor tomorrow."

"I have a tough time with kids. It's not that I don't like them, I just don't know how to get along with them. Oded hasn't stopped talking about kids since the day we met, and I just keep trying to buy time."

I ask if Oded is her husband, and I point out that she's always referred to him only as "my husband."

"I guess now I feel a little less sure that he's my husband."

"What do you mean?" I ask her.

All she says is, "It's complicated." Then she asks, "Do you think it'll keep raining for a long time?" I remind her that she promised to tell me why she was going to disappear, and she nods and says she'll keep her promise but not today. "I hope tomorrow goes well. I hope you don't get fired," she says, and a second before she steps out into the rain she gives me a kiss on the cheek and wishes me a good weekend.

I keep standing in the doorway for a few minutes, thinking about Raviv, about the meeting tomorrow, about Akirov's husband, Oded, who is now a little less her husband, and about that kiss she gave me. It was a friendly sort of kiss, and it smelled like tuna fish. The rain is coming down harder, and when I get sick of waiting, I walk out into it.

I don't wake up till four the next day. On days when I don't have to be at work, I don't set my alarm clock. On my phone I see a text message from Mom saying it'll just be the two of us for dinner because my brother is going away for the weekend with a woman he got set up with at work. She puts three exclamation points at the end of the message, like a sixteen-year-old girl. She's always dreaming about the day when my brother will re-marry. Somehow she's managed to convince herself that all the pissed-off bitterness that Hagai keeps vomiting on us comes from loneliness, and that the minute he finds someone who's willing to put up with him, he'll turn into a prince. The good news from my perspective is that I won't have to see him this evening. Then there's another blank message from Maor. I try to call him but his phone is off, so I leave a voice mail.

My mom makes an even more awesome dinner than usual—four courses, and for dessert, a layer cake from a recipe she found online. She's happy because of Hagai, and her happiness is contagious. I drink a lot of wine and we talk about my dad, about missing him, but it's still a cheerful sort of conversation. My mom says she'd always hoped to live to see grandchildren, and that even though she's already been a grandmother for

ages, her dream is for me to have a child. She asks how my law-
yer girlfriend is, and I say everything's going great, and that
Iris actually likes kids, but she's a little anxious that she won't
know how to manage them, just like I am. "I'm in no hurry,"
Mom says with a smile, "I've been waiting for you for so long,
I can wait a little longer."

It rains all day on Saturday. I huddle under the covers,
watching horror flicks and chain-smoking what's left of the
crappy pot Avri sold me a month ago. Maor's cell phone is still
off but he calls in the evening. He says the meeting didn't go
well. "You told Rosner that a kid brought a lighter to school
and caused problems, and that was why you didn't notice Liam
was gone—why did you do that? She brought it up it at the
meeting, and the principal talked to Yuri and started poking
around. The kid said the lighter was yours, and Yuri told the
principal he was the one who put out the fire. So, bottom line,
now you're a liar." He pauses, waiting for me to say something
in my defense. But I have nothing to say and I can't be bothered
anyway. "Rosner and the principal are both pissed off, and it
turns out that Gavri, the redhead kid who was punching Liam,
his grandfather's something senior in the Ministry of Education, so they can't kick him out of school. Rosner was raring to
go, she wants blood. So, long story short, I told them you're
done. Don't show up at work tomorrow. Call me in early March
and I'll leave you a check at the school office with however
much I owe you for February. And dude, next time you lie?
Use your brains. So long." Maor hangs up on me, and I feel

pretty fine about that. I didn't have anything smart to say on the occasion of my termination: it's not like it was some toast where you have to make a speech and then they give you a watch. Tomorrow I'll go look for another job. Maybe bartending. Night hours are better for me, and free liquor is just as good as meatballs in tomato sauce. It's insulting to be fired, there's no getting around that. To hear someone tell you you're not good enough is never a good feeling. But doing that work for 2,800 shekels a month wasn't something I could keep up for much longer anyway. I wonder if any of the kids will miss me when I don't turn up on Sunday.

At three a.m., Avri texts me: "Awake?" Like I'm his fuck buddy or something. On the phone he tells me his friend just arrived from Amsterdam with some good stuff. "Primo fresh," he says excitably, "he just shat it out. Should I run you over some?" By four he's at my place, and I use what's left from Akirov's two grand to buy eight grams. Avri tells me it's called Pineapple Crush, because this stuff is so strong that if you smoke enough of it, you can fall in love with a pineapple. After his passionate speech we smoke a bowl, and I don't fall in love with anything, but I do fly far, far away in my mind: I think about Raviv, and about that little stinker Liam, and about Liam's mom in her pink sweats who probably didn't give birth to him but just shat him out like Avri's friend shat out the Pineapple Crush for us. Then I think about Raviv some more, growing old and then becoming a baby again like that dwarf jellyfish; but mostly I think about Akirov and Oded, her slightly-less-so husband, and about how she's pretty much the only ray of light in my life, and now that's going to disappear, too. I'm so baked that I don't even notice Avri leaving, and sometime after the garbage truck finishes its round on my block, I fall asleep.

I get up just in time to shower, roll a joint, and bike to the promenade. The rain and wind have stopped, and there's finally going to be a real sunset. Akirov's already waiting on our bench. She finished work early. The first thing she does is ask about Maor and the meeting on Friday, and I tell her I got fired, and that maybe it's better that way. "Now you're my only employer," I say, as I pull a joint out of my Noblesse pack, "and that's why I've decided to take this business a little more seriously from now on. Check out the sunset I arranged for you!" It really is a beautiful one, and Akirov sits there silently, probably trying to come up with something comforting to say. I tell her that not only is there a premium sunset today, but premium pot, too. I tell her about Avri and the Pineapple Crush, but I skip the shitting part. The truth is, I've been smoking pot for twenty years and I've never had anything this good. After a few tokes you're absolutely flying.

We stay on the bench well after the sun has gone down, and I remind her again that she promised to tell me why she was disappearing. She looks at me with her clever green eyes. She's stoned out of her mind but she's still scrutinizing me. She smiles sadly and says she's also leaving her job, and that it's ending badly for her, too. Her law firm represents a few organized-crime families, and with one of them, it wasn't just legal advice—the firm was helping them launder money. We're talking tens of millions, and lots of important people are involved. But she wasn't. She found out by accident, and like an idiot she went to the police. When she did that, she didn't realize the extent of it. She thought she'd discovered a onetime transaction, which only one of the partners was involved in. By the time they figured out how serious it was, she couldn't back out. Now she's a state witness. She goes to work every day like everything's normal, eavesdrops and gathers material, and soon, when the whole thing blows up, she'll be out of here—they'll put her in the witness-protection program and give her a new identity overseas. Even she doesn't know where. "Oded told me yesterday," she said, attempting to sound calm, "that he's not coming with me. He's very close to his family and he's not up for disappearing."

"I'll come with you," I say, and I suddenly take her hand. "I'll come with you, wherever it is. I love surprises."

"This shit really is powerful," she says, laughing.

"Yeah, but regardless, I'd be happy to come. You're my only employer here, and when you leave, that'll be over, too. A new place? A new beginning? I could really get behind that. Just imagine if they put us on a tropical island! Every morning I'll climb up a tree and crack open a coconut for you."

"You're really into this!" She laughs some more. "It's too bad we can't switch."

"I don't want to switch." I start getting a little choked up now. "I want you."

She bites her lower lip and nods. Except it's not an "I know" nod, but more of an "I want you too" nod. And then comes this long second that the world has cleared away for us so we can kiss. But I'm too worked up to just kiss her. My stoned brain is too busy imagining us together, with different names, in a different place.

The second is over faster than I thought it would be. She stands up and smiles awkwardly and says she came to say good-bye because the timeline has changed: they're picking her up at ten tonight, and she has to say good-bye to her husband and her sister, who doesn't know anything about all this. I stand up, too, still trying to comprehend how I could have let that second evaporate, and she gives me one of those ordinary American-type hugs and says I'm a special person, which is something almost all the girls who wouldn't sleep with me said.

"Don't tell anyone, okay?" she says while she hails a cab. "Even after it all comes out. Promise? That'll only get me in trouble. And you."

I nod quickly and a minute later she's gone.

I bike home, still wicked high, and all the stoplights and the headlights and the cars honking mingle together in my head and it feels like a huge dance floor. The whole city looks happy—too happy. The munchies set in and I stop at the Yemeni falafel guy's stand on Nordau. Tomorrow Akirov starts her new life in a faraway place, without a husband and with a different name. It sounds like the beginning—or maybe the end—of a fairy tale. I believe she'll be happy there, wherever it may be, even if it's without me. Someone else will pick coconuts for her. Or she'll pick them herself. Wherever they send her, I hope it's somewhere warm. Every time I passed her a joint and our hands touched, her fingers felt cold.

EVOLUTION OF A BREAKUP

———

At first we were a cell. Then an amoeba, then a fish, and after a very long and frustrating era we became a lizard. That was the era when, as we recall, the earth felt soft and unsteady beneath our feet, so we climbed a tree. Up there in the treetops we felt secure. At some point, we climbed down and started walking upright and speaking, and as soon as we began speaking, we just couldn't stop. After that, we watched a lot of TV; it was a fantastic era. We always laughed in the wrong places, and people stared and said, "What's so funny?" And we didn't even bother answering—that's how little we cared. We promised ourselves we'd find a job we'd love, and when that didn't work out we settled for a job we didn't hate, and we felt lucky, and then unlucky, and then lucky again. And suddenly our parents were dying. Then they died. A second before they departed we held their hands really tight and told them we forgave them for everything. Everything. And our voices broke when we said that, because we weren't convinced we were telling the truth and were afraid they could sense it. Less than a year after that, our son was born, and he also climbed a tree and felt secure up there, and he came down at some point, too, and went off to college. Then we were left alone and it started getting cold. Not like it was that other time, eons ago, when we hid in burrows and peered out while the dinosaurs froze to death, but still cold. And we went to an acting class because our friends said it would be good for us. They gave us a series of improv exercises, and in the first one we poisoned each other; in the second, we cheated on each other; and in the third, the instructor, who spoke English with a heavy, indistinct accent, said, "Now switch partners." And within seconds it wasn't us anymore, it was just me. The new woman who was my partner said, "Let's do a sketch where you're a baby and I give birth to you and nurse you and protect you from all evil." And I said, "Sure, why not?" But by the time she'd finished giving birth to me and nursing me and protecting me from all evil, our time was up and the instructor with the strange accent asked if the exercise had brought back any primeval memories; and I said it hadn't, because I didn't want to admit that it had brought back ancient memories, from millions of years ago, from before we even emerged from the water. Afterward, at home, we got into an argument over something really dumb and had the biggest fight we'd ever had since we were created. We yelled and cried and broke things, the kinds of things that if you'd asked us a day earlier we'd have told you were unbreakable. Then we packed up our stuff in a suitcase and shoved whatever didn't fit in the suitcase into plastic grocery bags, and we dragged all that behind us like homeless people to the apartment where a very wealthy friend of ours lived, and he put a sheet out on his plush sofa for us. The friend told us that it might seem like the end of the world now, but by morning all the rage and hurt feelings would melt away and everything would look different. And we said no, something had been broken, something had been torn apart, something we would never be able to mend or forgive. The friend lit a cigarette and said, "Okay, maybe so. But can I just ask—why are you always talking in the plural?" Instead of answering, I just looked around and realized I was alone—I mean completely alone.